Three Women of Liverpool

HELEN FORRESTER was born in Hoylake,
Cheshire, the eldest of seven children, and
Liverpool was her home for many years until
she married. For the past twenty-seven years she
and her husband and their son have made their
home in Canada, in Edmonton, Alberta.
Together they have travelled in Europe, India,
the United States and Mexico.

The three volumes of Helen Forrester's auto-
biography are also published by Fontana, as is
her novel, *Liverpool Daisy*.

Available by the same author in Fontana

Twopence to Cross the Mersey
Liverpool Miss
By the Waters of Liverpool
Liverpool Daisy

HELEN FORRESTER

Three Women of Liverpool

FONTANA/Collins

First published by Robert Hale Ltd. in 1984
First issued in Fontana Paperbacks 1984

© Helen Forrester 1984

Made and printed in Great Britain by
William Collins Sons and Co. Ltd, Glasgow

Author's Note

The author would like to thank very much the Institute of Oceanographic Sciences, Bidston Observatory, Birkenhead, the Liverpool Record Office of the Brown, Picton and Hornby Libraries, her brothers and sister, and many friends and acquaintances for supplying her with much useful information on the subject of the great May blitz on Liverpool.

It should be pointed out that this is a novel, and the sailors' canteen, the situations and the characters are imaginary. Whatever similarity there may be of name, no reference is made or intended to any person living or dead.

In the spring of 1941, Admiral Erich Raeder wrote a memo to the Führer of the German Reich, Adolf Hitler. It said:

"An early concentrated attack on Britain is necessary, on Liverpool, for example, so that the whole nation will feel the effect."

THURSDAY 1 MAY 1941

He felt better, more sure of himself, now he was back in Liverpool and had a ship again. He had a new identity card safely tucked into the old wallet his father had found for him; it was surprising how naked you felt without a piece of paper to say who you were. Robert Owen, deckhand and fiancé of Emma Thomas, once more officially existed.

The clothing the Red Cross lady had found for him, to replace his lost kit, fitted well; the brown leather jacket would keep the wind out like nothing else would. He had had his faded blond hair cut in honour of his date with Emmie and he had a present for her in the brown paper carrier he was holding. His legs had stopped shaking.

Panic had, once more, struck him when, earlier that morning, he had entered the crowded Mercantile Marine office in search of a new set of papers and a new ship. At the thought of going to sea again, he had for a moment turned to jelly. He had not really walked to the huge mahogany counter; he had been nearly lifted off his damaged feet and edged towards it by the heaving, shouting mass of drunken seamen, all trying to get attention.

The clerk on the other side of the wide counter, a pimpled youth young enough to be his son, had been unexpectedly understanding of the tall, drained-looking deckhand in front of him.

"Two days on a raft, floating around in the Channel?" he had queried incredulously. "I'd have thought there was enough shipping down there that they would have spotted you in a few minutes."

"It's a lot o' water." Robert had tried to sound nonchalant. "Corvette out of Southampton picked me up." Again, he felt the ghastly fear that his hands would lose their grip on the raft and he would slide off and drown. "I were the only survivor." Try as he would, his voice still held a quiver.

"You were lucky."

"Aye, I suppose. Anyway, t' doctor says me feet'll be all right now. He signed me off yesterday. It were the cold water that effected 'em."

"Cold can do some rotten things to you," agreed the clerk. He chewed the end of his stub of pencil and ran his finger down a list. "There's the *Marakand* loading in No. 2 Huskisson. They're short a deckhand. How about it?"

To a fisherman who, until his last disastrous voyage, had always worked in his father's smack, one ship was as good as another, so he took the clerk's proffered fountain pen and shakily applied his signature where the boy pointed with his finger. A ship was a ship, and if he were going to marry Emmie he needed the money. If he did not go to sea, he would be called up for the army – at fourteen shillings a week. Better the devil you knew than the one that you did not.

Afterwards, until he got a better grip on himself, he stood on the handsome steps of the old Customs House, his hands in his pockets, the brown carrier bag swinging from his wrist. Beside him, legs astride, hands behind his back, stood the huge policeman who kept order amongst the tough clientele of the Mercantile Marine office. The sun lit up the long row of medal ribbons on his chest, but failed to soften a face with an expression that could have quelled an angry regimental sergeant-major. However, he said very cordially to Robert, "Nice mornin'. Ready for off agen?"

As Robert nodded affirmatively, the nervous twitch of his right eye was not lost on the constable and his expression returned to its usual grimness. Poor devil. Sent to sea again before he's fit, I'll bet me life. Just like the last war. He turned again to Robert and added, as if to offer some comfort, "You know, you're sometimes safer at sea than you are in Liverpool, these days, what with the air raids and all."

"Could be," Robert agreed, and then plunged down the steps, head bent to the wind, to make his way towards the gangway of the floating dock from which the ferry boats sailed across the river Mersey. There, he would meet Emmie.

With subs as numerous as cockroaches waiting for you once you'd crossed the bar, any minute could be your last. But this was also true of the hapless civilian. Air raids had been uncomfortably frequent all winter, and it worried him deeply that Emmie lived in Toxteth, within a half a mile of the much pounded dock area.

This was no way of thinking, he told himself crossly. He began to whistle firmly and winked at a very pregnant girl with a small child wrapped in her shawl. She sniffed and turned her face away from him. He grinned. Nothing like a Merseyside woman. As pretty as they come, like his Emmie with her soft voice with its Welsh inflections – and her warm body, surprisingly flexible for a middle-aged woman.

She was waiting, her face turned towards the multitude of shipping on the glittering river. A plain

13

navy skirt flapped against thin legs and she hugged a heavy blue cardigan against her chest, while the breeze whipped at her brown curls.

"It'll ruin me set before he ever comes," she muttered despondently and tried to smooth her ruffled locks. With her long, thin face and straight, determined-looking nose made pink by the fresh air, she appeared to the casual observer to be a nondescript woman approaching middle age. But Robert Owen was certain that she was the best thing that had happened to him in his entire life.

His mother, who wholly approved of her, said that the best thing that had ever happened to Emmie was that both her parents had finally died and had thus set her free.

"Like livin' in a box all her life, poor lass," she had told her son. "Now mind you give her some freedom, share with her, like. Too many women are nought but slaveys."

He had grinned and kissed her plump rosy cheek and had promised.

While Emmie waited, she thought again of the spate of wrath which she had, that morning, suffered from her sister-in-law, Gwen Thomas; and she wondered how much longer she could endure living with her. The moment she was married she would move out and find a room on the other side of the river, a room which she could make into a little home for Robert between voyages, until the war was over and they could hope for a better place.

Gwen had been furious that Patrick, the eldest of the family which lived next door, had shot an arrow through the glass of the Thomases' back bedroom window. Then, instead of being suitably apologetic, he had calmly asked for his arrow back. Emmie had burst into laughter at the sheer nerve of the lad, and this had set Gwen off on one of her lectures about responsibility and morality, which Emmie had endured with gritted teeth. What on earth had her brother, David, ever seen in the woman? A skinny, nagging ferret, she was.

She suddenly caught sight of Robert. Gwen was immediately forgotten and she ran towards him along the gently heaving dock, her whole body aching to hold him and be held by him.

Later, when he broke it to her that he would be sailing again in a day or two, she stroked the side of his face, as if to imprint on her memory every line of it. She touched the heavy blond brows and the tobacco-stained moustache. "Dearest Robbie," she whispered, "come back safe. I can't live without you." She snuggled closer. "You know, I never had a proper sweetheart before – I never had the time or the chance."

His lips curved mischievously under his moustache. "I know," he replied. "It were the biggest shock of me life when I realised it. Did I hurt you?"

Her thin white face was suddenly scarlet. "No – well, not much." She bit her lips, and then asked shyly, "Did you mind? Me not being at all experienced, like?"

"Nay, luv." He stood up suddenly from their seat on the top deck of the ferry and pulled her to her feet. "It were the nicest thing that ever happened to me – as if you'd been waiting for me." He held her closer. "But I can tell you, my girl, you were a real fast learner, you were."

"Well, at least I'm clean – no disease, I mean." She laughed self-consciously, her lower lip between her teeth. Then she looked at him wickedly out of the corner of her eyes, a plain woman suddenly made pretty.

ii

Emmie mechanically handed twopence to the plump, untidy clippie and received her tram ticket. Now Robert was about to sail, she felt deserted, unbelievably alone. At 39, she had never expected to marry; at that age one was on the shelf. She had many times told herself that such things were not for everyone; and she had done her best to ignore her inward longings, which could make nights a sleepless misery. She had had to try to be happy that she had nursed both her parents until they died. Then, when suddenly she was free of them, she had believed that she was too old for anything but more work. Domestic work, at that.

As she sat down on the slatted wooden seat of the tram, she asked herself bewilderedly whether it was really only four months since her father had died of heart failure. He had been a regular soldier, injured in the First World War, during army manoeuvres in 1915, and subsequently confined to a wheelchair for the rest of his life. And then, within a week, her mother who had been bedridden with arthritis for twenty-three years, had followed him, as if her reason for living had gone.

With both of them to nurse, no wonder I hadn't even time to wink at the milkman or gossip with the neighbours, thought Emmie. No time – and no money, to make myself look nice enough to find a husband. She closed her eyes, as she remembered all the lifting of them, the washing for them, the repulsive tasks of caring

16

for people well-nigh helpless. And her father forever filthy-tempered and her mother so fretful and in such dire pain.

Being Mrs Forster-Harrington's daily cleaning lady and cook had been rough, too, though her grand Victorian house had been very conveniently close to Emmie's tiny row house. Every morning, since the age of thirteen, she had run backwards and forwards from it and thus earned a little to augment her father's army pension, worried all the time that while she was away her father might fall out of his chair by the window or her mother might need her chamber pot. For twenty-six years she had stoically polished and scrubbed the house, through wars and Depression, until she knew every niche in the carved newel posts, every crack between the slate kitchen tiles. She did it while kind old Mrs Forster-Harrington, dressed in black silk, sat in her drawing room like Queen Victoria and mourned the death in 1918 of General Sir Alfred Forster-Harrington.

"Gone a bit soft in the head, she had, but proper kind for all that," Emmie had confided to Robert. "When I think on it, I were real lucky to have a job – so many didn't have one. But it were all work, Robbie. I never had a minute for meself. I never been to the pictures till you took me."

"Didn't they have any friends?" asked Robert incredulously. "To visit them, while you went out?"

"Not they. Me mam always said as soldiers often don't make many friends 'cos they move so much. Years ago, one or two serving men come to see me dad for a little while – but, you know, they went away – and some of them was killed in the war." She paused, and then added, "And they was both so short-tempered, they put people off, like."

After her mother's funeral, her brother, David, his wife, Gwen, and their sly, gangling 13-year-old daughter, Mari, all decorously clothed in black, had come back to Emmie's house. They had sat drinking tea in the living room, while Emmie wept out to David her fears for herself. She was panic-stricken that she did not earn enough to pay the rent and keep herself.

Gwen had sat silently sizing up the furniture in the tiny room. It's good, she had reflected. Can't buy that kind of stuff nowadays, particularly since the war began. Me best dishes would look great on the Welsh dresser. Young Mari, who had occasionally visited her grandparents in the front bedroom, had told her that there, also, the furniture was big and shiny and, therefore, probably good; David had said that the dead couple had inherited practically all of it from their parents. Now, David should inherit it, since he was the eldest; but if Emmie continued to live in her father's house, Gwen knew that David would never take the furniture from her.

While he listened to his sister's woes, David Thomas had stirred his tea with slow turns of the tin spoon. He felt tense and tired in his black Sunday suit and stiff white collar, and curiously breathless. He felt little sense of loss at his parents' death. His father had bullied him and his mother had been a nagger, though he felt sorry that she had had so much pain. Their death had, however, reawakened a strong sense of guilt regarding Emmie. He had berated himself that she had carried the whole load of his parents' invalidism, and Gwen, here, had done nothing whatever for them. He ought to have pushed Gwen harder, to take an occasional turn, so that Emmie could have gone out a bit. Emmie wasn't a bad looking woman and she had a real sweet manner with her – maybe got it from that Forster-Harrington woman. Given a chance, she might have married, and then he would not have had her on his hands now – though how any husband of hers would have put up with his parents, he could not imagine. Anyway, on his hands she was, and he knew he had to do something to get her started again.

With a slow ponderous movement, he put his spoon down in the saucer and rubbed the dark jowls of his face, while he looked out of the corner of his eye at his virago of a wife.

"Maybe I could go into service – Mrs Forster-Harrington might be glad to have me live in, now she's so old," Emmie sobbed, her pointed nose red from weeping.

"Nay. You're free now. You can do better'n that," her brother replied heavily. He was not going to see her thrown into the kind of jail that living-in domestic service could be. She'd had enough. She deserved better. "With the war on, there's a lot more work around for women now." He took a large breath and steeled himself, as he turned to Gwen. "She could have our middle bedroom for a while – till she got settled, like," he suggested.

Gwen sucked her teeth and turned a scornful glance at the dishevelled Emmie. Who wanted a plaster saint in the house? Another person to cook for?

But her husband's face reflected a stubbornness which had defeated her many a time in their married life, a woodenness which sometimes reminded her of

19

his father. She stared back at him uneasily.

David added, "She'll get work soon enough and then she can pay her shot, couldn't you, Emmie?"

Emmie gave a long shivering sigh and glanced uncertainly at Gwen. Gwen had, for the moment, put on her chapel expression, as Mari called it, a thoroughly virtuous look. It had suddenly been made clear to her how she could acquire her parents-in-law's furniture with a minimum of infighting.

"Aye," she agreed. "She can have the middle room – and there's space enough in the house, if I move our furniture round a bit, for the furniture from here."

Though very suspicious of Gwen's sudden acquiescence, Emmie said thankfully that, of course, she would pay. "And I could help you in the house," she added, as she wiped her eyes with the backs of her hands. Until she got on her feet, any company would be good company. And there was little Mari – she liked Mari.

Mari stopped munching seed-cake and unexpectedly interjected, "It would be nice if you could live with us, Auntie Emmie."

Emmie smiled waterily at her. From time to time, the child had come on her own, or with David, to see her grandparents, and Emmie had always spoiled her with a bit of cake or a sweet biscuit and a loving hug. To Mari, her aunt was easier to gossip with than her mother was. Mothers had a way of jumping on you, Mari had always thought, if you so much as said a word out of place.

With a satisfied smirk, Gwen rose, to indicate that they should leave. Once the furniture had been moved into her house, she would hold on to it; possession was nine points of the law. And if, in order to do this, she had to put up with a paying sister-in-law in the house for a while, it was cheap at the price; very different from having a couple of invalids wished on you, a fear which had haunted her all of her married life.

She sniffed. Despite the local gossips' accusations of neglect, David *had* visited his acerbic parents occasionally, and had spent good money on winter clothes and coal for them. Only Emmie had said thank you, according to David. And, she recollected bitterly, no one seemed to have ever given *her* any credit for getting by with that much less money.

iii

It proved simple to obtain work. After asking what experience she had, the employment exchange sent her to a sailors' canteen, set up in Paradise Street by a church group.

Stout, beaming Mrs Robinson, a volunteer who managed the place, was delighted to have an applicant willing to do washing up, clean lavatories and scrub floors. Furthermore, she liked the well-mannered, grey-eyed woman with a face as innocent as a nun's, yet old enough to keep young seafarers at bay.

"We have a lot of volunteers on the staff, but occasionally they don't turn up," she explained to Emmie. "Then we have to manage somehow, so we have four full-time paid people, two for each shift."

Emmie smiled and said she could cook, too. Mrs Robinson looked at the marvellous reference from the Honourable Mrs Forster-Harrington – and increased the wage offered by five shillings a week.

At seven the next morning Emmie was given a white overall and the prettiest flowered apron she had ever worn, and was sent across a small back yard to scrub two very dirty lavatories.

The yard was cobbled and was obviously much older than the buildings surrounding it; it had been adapted as a light well and was lined overhead with office windows. Little of the spring sunshine penetrated it; only a small square patch of sky far above hinted at the beauty of the day.

With her long, straight nose wrinkled in disgust, Emmie used up four pails of hot water and a whole bottle of pine disinfectant and, to the relief of the other members of the staff who had to use the ancient thrones, as well as the seamen, she had left them cleaner than they had been for half a century.

When she returned to the canteen itself, she saw that the front door was hospitably open, though round the entrance stood a wall of sandbags to protect it from blast. The two big windows facing the street had been pushed up; their panes had been criss-crossed with black tape, to minimise the danger of flying glass, and on either side big, old-fashioned shutters, their hinges well oiled, hung ready to be folded across the windows at night.

Two volunteers were wiping down the tables and chairs. They were both dressed in matching sweaters and cardigans, one in pink, the other in green. Over their tweed skirts they had tied flowered aprons similar to Emmie's. One had a string of pearls round her neck, the other a gold chain with a cross hanging from it. Though they were about the same age as Emmie, Emmie thought she had never seen two more beautiful young ladies. They greeted her cheerfully and asked her name; she did not dare to ask them their names.

Bringing with her a strong smell of sausages grilling, Mrs Robinson rushed in from the kitchen carrying a pile of clean ashtrays. "Put one of these on each table, Emmie," she ordered briskly.

"It's funny-peculiar how small things change your life," Emmie remarked to Mari later on. "All the happiness I've got came because I had to put an ashtray on a certain table. Proper queer, when you think on it."

As Emmie put down the last ashtray, two men, anxious for a late breakfast, swung themselves into chairs at the table. Both wore navy-blue turtleneck sweaters and shabby jackets over them. They grinned up at Emmie.

"Mornin', duck. What you got for brekkie?" The speaker must have been in his sixties, judging by his almost bald head fringed by tightly clipped white hair. Black eyes, like a friendly magpie's, surveyed her.

Emmie blushed slightly. "I don't know. I can smell sausages."

The other man was younger, fair-haired, with a full moustache tinged orange by tobacco smoke. He laughed, and Emmie's blush grew redder, because she felt she had given a stupid answer. Her fingers fidgeted with a corner of her flowered apron. After a second, he said to his companion, "It doesn't matter what it is, Dickie. I'm that hungry, I could eat an elephant. Had to wait hours at the bloody hospital, in spite o' being so early."

"Aye. Bring two plates of whatever's cooking," agreed his companion, taking a well-charred pipe out of his pocket and then opening up an oilskin tobacco pouch from another pocket.

Emmie flashed them a shy smile and fled to the kitchen. She reported anxiously to Mrs Robinson.

Mrs Robinson paused, a half-open packet of dried eggs in her hand. Then she chuckled. "Here, take a pencil and notebook from over there, and ask them whether they want tea or coffee, bread or toast, and would they like porridge to start with."

Flustered, Emmie snatched up the notebook, while Mrs Robinson called after her, "We've got scrambled eggs, sausages and baked beans."

Emmie waited, pencil poised, until the men looked up from their conversation. Behind her, other men rolled in with the typical sailor's gait, each man's head bent slightly forward, chin tucked in, from years of living in boats' confining spaces, where heads could be easily bumped. Coughing, hawking, talking, they scraped chairs back from the tables, while the volunteers advanced purposefully, notebooks in hand.

The man with the moustache watched her curiously, as she took his friend's order; when she turned to him she found herself facing rich blue eyes, narrowed as though used to staring into sunlight. The face was weatherbeaten, lined and filled with strain. He smiled at her and she lowered her eyes modestly, as she wrote the order down. Her mother had been warning her since the First World War about being forward with men. Not that she need have worried, thought Emmie. When you're keeping house you live in a daytime world of women, children and very old men. Even the tiny shops she had patronised had been largely run by women, and her parents had never allowed her to go out at night;

when she had once or twice protested at this, her father had, in a tremendous rage, shouted her down, threatened her with his stick and told her that it was bad enough that they were left alone in the mornings while she was with Mrs Forster-Harrington and went for the groceries. Many of her neighbours were equally tied to their homes, she knew, by a horde of children, the sick or the old, and by sheer lack of a penny of their own. She submitted.

This morning, she was being rapidly surrounded by an ever increasing crowd of lively, talkative men. It felt very strange, nervously exciting.

"Tea or coffee?" she inquired of her younger customer, forcing herself to look at him. He grinned, a slow, friendly smile, which made all the sun wrinkles on his face stand out. Her heart gave an uncomfortable bounce. "Tea," he replied, and then asked, "You new here?"

"Yes," she said shyly, smiled briefly and hurried back to the safety of the kitchen. A whole lot of questions about men tumbled into her mind. Here, this very morning, she was going to meet more men than she believed she had met in the whole of her desperately narrow existence, and she really knew very little about them.

When she was a young girl and her mother was still able to move around the house a little, she had not dreamed of being tied to her parents for the rest of her life. She had hoped for a handsome sweetheart in soldier's uniform, with fine legs bound up in puttees; but her parents had kept her rigidly reined in and, very soon afterwards, the horrible battles of the First World War had taken nearly all the young men of the district, and hardly any of them returned. "Round us, there must have been three girls to every man," she guessed, as through the day she trotted patiently backwards and forwards to the tables; and once she suddenly felt sick, as she realised that the same thing was going to happen to the young girls now hoping for a husband. The young lads were again going out to die. And for what? How many men in this very room would be alive twelve months hence?

The man with the moustache came again the next morning, this time for a cup of coffee and a bun. He sat at the same table. Dickie was not with him.

Emmie snatched her notebook out of her apron pocket and scuttled across the crowded room to take his order, afraid that one of the volunteers would get there first.

"Mornin'," she greeted him shyly, wondering what had brought her to him at a run. He was sitting with his elbows on the small round table, chin resting on clasped hands. At her voice, he glanced up quickly and smiled. Despite the smile, he looked drawn and very tired.

"We got a bit o' bacon," she whispered conspiratorialy. "Would you like some?"

He had already had breakfast with his parents, out at Hoylake, but he was delighted to be specially favoured. "Ah would," he said, the smile broadening into a grin.

When he took his cup of coffee from her instead of allowing her to lay it on the table, she noticed that his hand was not too steady. The cup wobbled in the ill-fitting saucer and then tipped over. He was deluged in coffee.

She whipped a tea towel from the belt of her apron and gave it to him to wipe himself down, while they had

26

a rueful laugh together. "Lucky your trousers is navy blue," she told him. "Stain won't show."

When she brought his bill, he asked her rather diffidently if she would like to go to the cinema with him the following night.

Gwen was scandalized. "At your age!" she exclaimed. "Lettin' yourself be picked up."

Mari had giggled, and said, "It's exciting for her, Mam." Her mother's look was sufficient to freeze her into silence and, with tight lips, the 13-year-old again bent her head over her knitting.

Shaken by a series of emotions she had never expected to be able to give range to, Emmie had turned appealingly to David.

"I'm free now," she said to him, a little break in her voice. "I'm goin' to enjoy meself as much as I can."

David folded his newspaper up carefully. "And so you should," he said, regardless of his wife's grim disapproval. "Be careful who you're with, that's all."

"He's a real nice fella," responded Emmie, looking defiantly at Gwen. Inwardly, she wondered what kind of a man she had drawn out of the pack. He was certainly nothing like her father. She was trembling with nervous anticipation, as, after tea, she washed her face and did her hair. Instead of her usual bun, she rolled her long hair over a shoelace tied round her head and the result was a smooth, neat roll which framed her face; she had got the idea from a women's magazine which Gwen subscribed to. As she tucked in a few precious hairpins to make sure the roll did not slip, she wondered frantically if he were married.

Now, homeward bound on the clanging tram, she reflected fondly on the memory of that first date. There had not been an air raid and they had laughed together as they stumbled round in the blacked out city. He had insisted on bringing her all the way home to her brother's house and he had actually kissed her before leaving her. With joy mixed with fear for his safety, she once more felt under her glove the small garnet-and-pearl ring which a couple of weeks back he had given her.

He had produced it shyly and had confessed when he had slipped it on to her finger, "I never thought much about getting married before – always seemed to be too much to do, fishing with me father. Prices was so bad we never made much – not enough for me to keep a wife as well. Being Methodists, me and me brothers didn't drink and we didn't dance, so we didn't meet too many womenfolk – a few neighbouring girls – but never anyone like you, Emmie. You're beautiful and I want you so bad."

They had lain in the damp April grass, amid the Meols sand-dunes, not too far from his home. Great rolls of barbed wire stretched along the beach, to protect it from possible invasion. The Home Guard, keeping their nightly watch, had left them undisturbed. Rumour had it that both the beach and the dunes were mined, but they forgot everything in their need for each other. While the sound of the waves rolling softly up the shore, and a silent sea mist drifting inland, cut them off for a little while from a world in torment, two gentle, deprived people found an ecstasy granted to few.

They lay for a long time in each other's arms, until Emmie giggled suddenly.

"I was thinkin'. Supposing I have a baby! It *could* happen, even at my age."

Robert had lifted his head and kissed her again. "Not to worry. It'll have a proper father. I wouldn't let you down, luv." He held her tightly, and then said, "If anything should happen to me before we can be married, and you're in trouble, go to me mam and dad. They'll take care of you."

"Oh, Robbie," she whispered with a sigh. "You have to come back safe."

"I'll do me best," he said, with a forced laugh. "But don't you forget. Me dad's earning enough now to keep you for a while."

She lay quiet for a moment, and then she said in a puzzled voice, "It's funny that it's taken a war to give us decent wages, isn't it?" She rolled over him until she was lying on top of him, her head on his shoulder, and then she sighed. "But I'd rather manage on poor wages and know you was safe." She felt him stir under her again and scrambled hastily to her feet. "Enough, luv, enough. I got to go to work on the morning. And you got to have the hospital check your feet again. The cold and wet you suffered on that raft must've been proper awful." She dusted down her skirt and buttoned up her blouse, looking down at him impishly. "But, you know, I wish your feet were still just a bit bad, so as we could have more time together before you have to go to sea again."

He had swung himself to his feet and caught her in his arms and kissed her long and hard. "Aye, luv, I don't want to go either."

Another time, while they sat on a bench underneath a chestnut tree in Sefton Park, she had told him about her life with her parents. He had marvelled at her patience and endurance. She had shrugged her shoulders and said, "I only did what a lot of single daughters have to

29

do – who else will look after people like that? Couldn't let them go into the workhouse. We could just manage if we all three lived together. But there wasn't nothin' left over for going to the pictures or suchlike, even if I'd had the time. We was lucky to have a low rent and something to eat each day. We'd have fair frozen to death some winters, if David hadn't bought some coal."

"It'll be easier from now on, luv," he had promised her. And she had felt indeed that a new life was unfurling for her as surely as the tiny leaves sprouting on the chestnut tree.

"Rialto Cinema," shouted the clippie, and Emmie came sharply back to the present.

iv

Gwen Thomas always averred that her life was never the same again after that young scoundrel, Patrick Donnelly from next door, had at dinnertime on Wednesday shot an arrow through the back bedroom window of their small row house.

"There was broken glass all over our Mari's bedspread. Ruined, it was," she complained angrily to Emmie and to her husband, David.

She was sick to death of her new, Irish next-door neighbours. A pack of sloths, she fumed. She had nearly choked when the 13-year-old boy had calmly knocked at her back door and had asked for his arrow back.

A small bundle of outrage, thin lips drawn back over blackened broken teeth, she had hissed back, "Arrow?

You ain't gettin' no arrow from me, young man. You're goin' to get a bill for seven bob for puttin' t'glass back, and I hope your dad gives you a good beatin'."

Large, calculating blue eyes, fringed with long black eyelashes, looked calmly back at her. "It were an accident, Mrs Thomas – and you could say it were blown out in the last air raid and get it mended easy." He grinned at her beguilingly, a grin that usually worked wonders with middle-aged lady teachers.

It did not work on Gwen Thomas. She wanted to strike him with the broom she was holding; but he was as tall as she was and heavily built for his age. She felt uneasily that he might hit her back. She shook a bony finger at him.

"And what good would that do me, beyond makin' a liar of meself?"

"T' city might do it for free."

She slammed the door in his face.

Bow in hand, he stood staring at the cracked black paint on the back door. All that fuss about a window, when any night the Jerries raided Liverpool hundreds of windows got broken. Old bitch.

On the way out of the tiny brick-lined yard, he gave the cages holding David Thomas's racing pigeons an angry shake. The pigeons fluttered madly round and round their prison in alarm. Next time he shot at a cat, he reckoned crossly, he should take a look at what else was in the line of flight. As his father often said, you live and learn.

"Patrick! Patrick! Coom 'ere. I want yer to go a message, afore you go back to school," he could hear his mother shouting from their kitchen. "Coom 'ere, afore I come after yez. Where are you?"

He dropped his bow into a corner behind the lavatory in the yard and slunk uneasily into the kitchen.

In her living room, Gwen sank on to the sofa, leaned back and flung a skinny arm across her chest. "He's started me palpitations, he has. Mari, luv, pour me another cuppa tea and bring the aspirin bottle."

Mari was just putting on her school blazer, preparatory to returning to school, but she obediently ran upstairs to her mother's bedroom to get the aspirin bottle and, on her return, poured a cup of tea from the aluminium teapot keeping warm on the hob in front of the fire.

"I don't suppose he meant to break the window, Mam," she pleaded, turning a thin, well-scrubbed face towards her mother who was lying back with her eyes closed.

Gwen ignored her plea. She shook a couple of aspirins out of the bottle, popped them into her mouth and swallowed them down with a gulp of tea. "Mind you come straight home," she told her daughter, without opening her eye. The girl slowly buttoned her blazer and, with a sour grimace towards her mother, she left for school. Palpitations! How come every time her mother fell into a fit of rage, it was called palpitations, and when she, Mari, was angry, it was called a sinful paddywack.

As she kicked a stone down the road towards school – her mother hated her to do anything so vulgar – she ruminated on the subject of Patrick. Though she was scared of him, she found him a fascinating subject for thought. Her school friends thought he was the handsomest boy in the neighbourhood and he was so excitingly wild – and a wicked Catholic, too. Only last week, at the end of the street, he had fought off three Protestant boys and left them all with bleeding noses. Cock of the walk, he was, thought Mari a trifle wistfully. But her mother's warnings about men had been drummed into her ever since she could stand, and while the other girls, Protestant and Catholic alike, giggled hopefully whenever they passed him, she held back and passed with eyes cast down, her satchel carried neatly on her back, to cover her long black plait so that boys could not pull it.

v

Emmie descended from the tram and walked briskly down a side street towards her brother's house. The wind sent bits of paper skittering before her, and a red-faced baby, which seemed to have got dust in its eyes, was wailing unhappily in a pram set outside one of the front doors. In a gutter, two small boys in brown woollen jerseys were quarrelling loudly over their coloured glass marbles.

"Evenin', Miss Thomas."

At the sound of the deep Irish voice, Emmie's lips clamped together. She half turned towards the lanky man in blue air raid warden's overalls, who had fallen into step with her. His battered old retriever, Sarge, nosed between them as if anxious not to be ignored, and she bent to stroke his dusty muzzle. "Evening, Mr Donnelly," she replied a little stiffly, uncertain how to treat him.

Patrick's father, with his shrieking wife and bevy of unwashed children, had been, according to Gwen, a no-good out-of-work until he had been made a warden. "Keeps fighting cocks, if you please. Says a bad shoulder keeps him out of the army, ha! For ever shouting at you to 'put that light out'. Never seems to miss the slightest chink in your blackout curtains. Thinks you're signalling to the Jerries if you so much as carry a candle down the yard when you got to go to the lavvie. Work? He lives the life of Riley."

For his part, Conor Donnelly regarded Gwen and David Thomas as worse than a packet of starch, with their highly polished and scrubbed house front, their ritual of Sunday clothes and chapel-going, their disapproval of little boys who sometimes got caught short and piddled on the pavement, and ate conny-onny butties while sitting on their adjacent front doorstep. Ellen Donnelly had expressed the opinion that, "Them holier-than-thou types is the worst. That Mari'll be in trouble with the boys in no time at all, at all."

Conor Donnelly could not imagine how anybody could endure such a regimented life, without even an occasional bout of drinking or fighting to break the monotony. Of course, since he had become an air raid warden he had had to mind himself a bit. He had to stay sober while on duty and be a bit careful when he was carrying stolen goods for a small group of friends who preyed on lorries serving the docks.

When he and his family had been bombed out in the previous autumn, the city had rehoused him in the empty row house next door to Mr High and Mighty David Thomas, plumber. That bombing had been a basketful, that had. Poor little Ruby, his eldest daughter, and old Sarge had been buried for nearly four hours. A bloody miracle that the rest of them had been at the pictures at the time.

Miss Thomas, now she was different. She was polite to his wife and sometimes she made jokes with the kids. On Easter morning she had filled Ruby's hands with toffees – must have given her most of her ration – to share with the other kids. She was a very quiet woman, he mused, but with a bit of encouragement from the right fella she might be more lively than she appeared. His face crinkled up in a grin, as she glanced up at him. He ventured a mild joke and was rewarded by a shy laugh.

Emmie forced herself to attend to what he was saying. With his face a polished mahogany from years of inadequate washing and his long, yellow teeth, he was an oddity to her; yet his sheer bouncing gaiety was infectious and she could understand why he had been chosen as an air raid warden – he would be a real tonic if you were in trouble.

They turned towards their adjoining front doorsteps. Conor pushed open his unlocked door, while she inserted her key into her brother's carefully burnished Yale lock. Before he entered, Conor turned to point up to the sky, where a few clouds were building and a slight haze was dulling the sunshine.

"Bit o' luck and them clouds'll form a nice cover afore midnight. Should mean no raid."

"Aye. It's been over quiet lately, hasn't it? Makes you wonder what's brewing."

Conor nodded agreement. "Well, keep yer fingers crossed."

"I got to work the late shift at the canteen tonight, so I'll be up and about anyways," Emmie confided.

As usual, the slam of the Donnelly's front door caused a slight shudder to pass through the Thomases' house and rattled the wooden signboard nailed to their door. The faded board announced *David Thomas, plumber, est. 1914. Prompt attention.*

The noise immediately brought Gwen Thomas out of the back kitchen. She clucked fussily, as clearly through the dividing wall came the sound of Ellen Donnelly's strident voice above the shriek of a child. Conor's voice rumbled back.

"Really! Slammin' t' door like that! Brings all the dust down. And me just finished cleaning." Red-ringed, faded blue eyes looked impatiently up at Emmie, as Gwen licked her finger and ran it along a ledge to pick up an offending grain of dust.

Emmie hung up her coat, gas mask and handbag on the hall peg. While she nerved herself to deal with Gwen, she picked up the floppy, brown carrier bag given to her by Robert. She was always anxious not to break up her tenuous housing arrangement by letting her bitter, pent-up resentment burst forth at Gwen's never having given her the slightest help with her parents. She was grateful for David's protection and did not want to move until she was married. Though she was now paying very adequately for her lodgings and she also helped Gwen in the house, Gwen never considered it necessary to thank her and was often barely civil.

Nothing annoyed Gwen more than dust and dirt and untidiness, and her shining, neat house indicated how successfully she dealt with them. Almost invariably wrapped in a black cross-over overall dotted with blue forget-me-nots, she was a bundle of muscles. Because she kept running her fingers through her greying red hair with its tight natural curl, it tended to stand up in a wild bush. Tonight it was in particular dissarray, indicating a trying day's battle with her household gods.

"'T' glazier hasn't got no glass for Mari's bedroom window," she grumbled, as she followed Emmie into the living room, where a cheerful fire blazed in an old-fashioned cooking range gleaming with blackleading; at its side, the brass tap of the hot water tank winked in the light of the darting flames.

David Thomas was seated in his armchair beside the fire, and he looked up from his perusal of the *Liverpool Echo*. "'Allo, la," he greeted Emmie, and then he said to his wife. "I'll nail a bit o' plywood over t' window when I've had me tea. It'll be safer for Mari than glass."

"Where *is* Mari?" inquired Emmie, smiling down at her brother.

"She's away out to tea with her friend, Dorothy." Gwen clicked her tongue and reverted to her grievance. "I'll teach that lad, even if his mam won't. He'll not get his arrow back." She continued to grumble, as she went through to the back kitchen. Emmie followed her with the carrier bag.

She interrupted Gwen's tirade, by saying, "Robbie set a line while the tide was out yesterday. He caught ten whiting and he's sent you two. They feel real heavy."

"That's proper kind of him, I'm sure," replied Gwen coldly. She seized a pot of boiled potatoes and deftly drained the water from them into the sink. Through the ensuing steam, she added with a sniff, "Being engaged to

37

a fisherman has its advantages, I suppose. T' fishmonger didn't have so much as a cod's head left today, by the time he got to me. Ever so long, the queue was."

"Well, there's the makin's of a nice dinner here," Emmie soothed.

"Humph," grunted Gwen. "Here, take the potatoes and put them on the table for me." She sighed. Provided Emmie could be prevented from taking her parents' furniture with her, she would be thankful when the woman got married and left. When the pieces had been moved into the house, nothing had been said as to the ownership; but Gwen burnished them determinedly; they were hers, because David was the eldest and should inherit.

What little Emmie said about the furniture indicated that she took it for granted that, since she had lived with it all her life, the furniture belonged to her. Besides, in the middle of a war, where else would she get furniture from for a home?

She had brought Robert home for tea one Sunday and Gwen had made it clear that she strongly disapproved of a woman of sober years suddenly marrying a man she had known less than four months. It did not occur to Emmie that Gwen had been smitten by a lingering envy of her blatant happiness, her obvious contentment.

"I must hurry," said Emmie, as they sat down to their meal. "I got to be in the canteen by seven. Mrs Robinson and the others were ever so kind about me engagement, giving me a bit of time off when Robbie was free."

Gwen responded tartly, "Well, I hope you're doing the right thing." She stirred her tea hard, in the hope of making half a teaspoonful of her sugar ration sweeten it adequately. She made a face when she sipped it. "Picking up a man like that don't seem like a good start to me."

Emmie ached to slap her.

"Now, Gwen," her husband warned. "Emmie got to know him in the canteen. That's not picking up. And he took her home to Hoylake to meet his mum and dad – quite proper. He's given her a nice ring, too."

Gwen shrugged her shoulders slightly and poured another cup of tea. Emmie kept her eyelids down and wondered if Gwen had ever been in love with poor David – or with anything except the shiny aspidistra in the front room or the bronze soldiers looking down at them from the living room mantelpiece.

To distract Gwen, David said, "I'll get me tools and do Mari's window."

That brought Gwen back to her favourite complaint – the Donnellys. "We ought to have moved from here years ago – the whole of Toxteth's gone to pot. The minute Mrs Tasker died next door I knew we'd never get decent neighbours again."

"House were empty for months. T' landlord held out for too high a rent." David gritted his teeth as he pushed away his empty plate.

"Oh, aye. And how does he pay seventeen shillings a week on an air raid warden's wages, I'd like to know. Maybe it's true that he's hand in hand with a gang o' dock thieves."

"Gwen!" David was shocked. "That's just idle gossip. Because he sometimes has lipsticks or silk stockings for sale? He could buy 'em easy from a merchant seaman on the New York run. It don't make 'im a thief."

The sharp wail of the air raid siren made David jump. He had been washing himself in the kitchen sink, in preparation for going to bed, and he stood in his undervest and trousers while he dried the back of his neck. He was numb with fatigue after a long day working on the intricacies of the plumbing of the Royal Infirmary, and he felt again a small, choking pain in the middle of his chest, a pain that had been bothering him occasionally for a couple of weeks.

"Blow them," he muttered, and hastily finished drying himself.

He leaned over the sink to pull back the blackout curtain and look out of the window. There was enough moonlight to cast a shadow of the house across the back yard. Behind the neighbouring chimneys, searchlights suddenly sent seeking fingers across a starry sky. It was much too light for safety. He dropped the curtain into place, making the flame of the candle on the drainboard dance, as Gwen came hurrying from the living room. She carried a steaming kettle in one hand, and the warning had obviously flustered her.

"For goodness' sake, get your dressing-gown on and something on your feet. We'll have tea on the cellar steps. What a nuisance they are."

As she flung two teaspoonsful of tea into the pot, she went on anxiously, "Our Mari's not in yet, from

Dorothy's. She's real late. I'll have to have a word with that young lady."

"I could go and fetch her," David offered, without much conviction.

"No. It'd just mean two of you out in the flak. You get out the blankets and cushions and take them on to the cellar steps, while I do the tea tray." She jumped suddenly, as the steady boom-boom of anti-aircraft fire made the windows rattle. Sometimes the guns sounded more menacing than the bombs did.

David would have been thankful to crawl into bed and risk being blown out of it. He did not feel, however, that he could go to bed while Mari was still not home, so he obediently arranged the cushions on the cellar steps, for them to sit on. With the slope of the staircase overhead, this spot offered good protection and the least likelihood of being crushed.

With a sigh, he sat down and arranged a blanket over his knees. While Gwen held the tea tray a little high, he tucked another blanket round her. He took the candle from the tray and set it on a small shelf above their heads. Gwen scolded, "Be careful, stupid. You'll upset the tray." She stirred the pot balanced uncertainly on the tray on her lap, while he listened for the battery to start firing in nearby Princes Park; the sound would indicate to him how close the raiders were. Beyond the rumble of more distant guns, however, all he heard was Donnelly's front door slam. Likely, Donnelly was in for a busy night.

Gwen's lips curled. "That'll be him goin' down to the wardens' post. Bangin' the door, as usual. No manners, that man."

Their own front door slammed. Quick footsteps ran

along the narrow, linoleumed passage, then stumbled through the dark living room and into the kitchen.

"That you, Mari? Come on down, quick now."

Mari was panting, as she whipped a cushion off the shelf and almost slithered down the concrete steps, her long bare legs flashing white in the candlelight.

She sat down close to her mother. Like many families seeking refuge in this safest corner of the house, they always sat very tightly together, so that if the building was hit they either died or survived together.

Gwen felt her trembling and lifted down the candle to have a closer look at her. The girl's face was blenched and her eyes stared unblinkingly at her mother from behind the candle flame.

"There, there, luv. No need to be scared. You're safe home now," she told the girl quite gently.

Her father turned towards her and added reassuringly, "It don't sound as if they're interested in the south end of the town tonight."

Above them, a number of aeroplane engines throbbed increasingly loudly.

"They'll be some of ours," David declared authoritatively. "Always know the difference by the sound o' the engines."

His words were immediately belied by a shrieking whistle passing over them. Instinctively, they ducked and flung their hands over their heads for protection. The tea tray on Gwen's lap rocked perilously. There was a moment of silence: then a deafening explosion which shook the whole house above them. They waited, like rabbits hiding in a thorn bush from a fox. A piece of plaster plopped from the ceiling on to the tray, and a cloud of thin dust enveloped them.

Mari buried her face against her mother's bony legs and whimpered in terror. The next bomb in the rack would hit them; she knew it. It would be a judgment on her for what she had allowed Patrick Donnelly to do to her.

He had been bothering her for weeks, touching her when she passed him, holding her against the wall of the alley one day, when she had run down it to visit Dorothy; not hurting her, just making her feel funny when he pressed himself against her. It had been most funny-peculiar, because, despite all her mother's warning about not letting a man come near her, she had wanted him to remain close. Perhaps the warning didn't apply to boys, she argued to herself.

Tonight, he had pushed her into a street air raid shelter, which nobody used except as a urinal. He had held her tightly against the wall and her silent struggles had been of no avail against his considerable weight. When in scared despair, she had stopped wriggling, he had lifted her skirt and gently stroked between her legs. And she knew now that she was on her way to hell. It had felt wonderful, incredible; and he had laughed when, not understanding the driving impulse, she had put her arms round him. He had said it was nothing to what he could do. If that was nothing, she decided without really knowing why, it was a good thing that the air raid warning had begun to shriek and that they had both run for home.

Now the bombs were falling all around her. God must be very angry with her.

"Incendiaries! Incendiaries!" Conor Donnelly could be heard, calling his firewatchers to the street.

Despite his wife's protests, David insisted on going

43

out in his dressing-gown to check his roof, back and front. He came back very soberly and hauled the blanket round himself again. "Looks like the whole town's alight. Hope our Emmie's all right." Then to his crouching daughter, he said, "Don't take on so, Mari. Everything's going to be all right. We're quite safe here on the steps."

You don't know what a wicked daughter you've got, thought Mari, not lifting her head from her mother's knee. God could do anything to us tonight.

viii

As the guns in Princes Park began to roar, Ellen Donnelly finished spreading the washing on her wooden airer in her living room and then heaved the heavy rack up to the ceiling again and tied the rope firmly to hold it there. The clothes began to drip depressingly onto the rag rug below and onto the otherwise bare floor. A few droplets reached baby Michael asleep in a battered easy chair. She edged the chair away from under the rack and flung her black woollen shawl over the sleeping child.

There was a quick patter of bare feet on the stairs, and her eldest daughter, Ruby, still in her clothes, dashed into the room. She was brought up short by the sight of her mother seating herself calmly on a wooden chair in front of the fire.

"Mam, shall I bring Brendy and Nora down? The guns sound awful." Her voice was tightly constricted, as she tried to control her panic. After the dreadful experience of being buried in the ruins of their former home, the sound of the air raid warning always brought her close to a bout of hysterics. Her breath came in tight gasps and, from under a fringe like a Skye terrier's, eyes gleamed with tears.

"Aye, luv. Coom 'ere." Her mother held out a stout red arm to her and thankfully the skinny 12-year-old cuddled close to her heavy breast. "It ain't likely we'll be bombed again."

The guns continued to growl and, after a minute, Ellen said, "Let's have a look-see outside. Then we'll decide if we should bring t' kids down." She rose, and went to the front door, Ruby trotting closely behind her for comfort.

With a strong, red hand on either door-post, she leaned out as far as she could. The wind caught her untidy mop of shoulder-length hair and flapped her long black skirt. Metronomic searchlights flicked back and forth across the sky as if to time the drumming guns, and high in the heavens a bright flare floated gently; it silvered the slate roofs of the close-packed houses, gave a halo to a church spire and outlined the solid mass of a nearby tenement building.

"Reckon they're doin' Wallasey and Birkenhead tonight," she opined comfortingly. "Quite away from us. We'll let the kids rest for a bit. You come and sit by the fire with me and we'll have a drop of your dad's whiskey."

Ruby did not like the taste of whiskey, but since the disastrous raid which had robbed them of their home, her mother had often given her a teaspoonful of it, and it made her feel better. Now, she went to the dying fire to warm her bare feet, while her mother tried to guess where Donnelly's latest hiding-place for the bottle might

45

be. In such an empty home there were not many places to look.

She found it on the windowsill, behind the blackout curtain, and she sat down while she eased out the cork. Ruby came to lean against her. The glow from the fire lit up their faces, as they solemnly took a sip each from the bottle. Then Ellen took a good gulp, and gasped as it caught her throat. She laughed and set down the bottle under her chair and again put her arm round Ruby.

The front door was flung open. Patrick strolled slowly in, determined to show that he was not afraid of air raids. A cool breeze followed him in.

"What you bin up to?" Ellen inquired truculently. "You're lookin' too pleased with yourself by far."

"Haven't bin doin' nothin'." The satisfied grin on his face belied his words, but she knew from experience that she would get no more out of him.

A screaming whistle overhead wiped the grin from Patrick's face, but, hands in pockets, he stood his ground, while Ruby clung shrieking to her mother. Blast swung the front door hard open and shook the old house. The blackout curtains billowed like sails in a sudden gust. A mass of soot descended the chimney, obliterated the fire and covered all of them in black dust. Little Michael, covered by his mother's thick shawl, continued to sleep, but from upstairs came frightened howls.

Ellen wiped the soot off her mouth. "God's curse upon the buggers!" she cried, and bent down to reach for the whiskey bottle.

A piece of debris landed on the roof with a sharp crump; then, for a moment, unearthly quiet.

A nerve-racking clatter in the street and the familiar

sound of her husband's running feet caused Ellen to burst out again, "Incendiaries, blast 'em!"

Patrick went to the door. The darkness was broken all along the street by sparks hissing from the small, vicious fire bombs. Dark shadows carrying sandbags ran to dowse the scary, sizzling devils, and one or two bravely tried to put them out by holding dustbin lids over them. Patrick seized one of the sandbags in the hall and ran gleefully out to help.

Opposite, a furious Bridget Mahoney flung up the empty frames of her bedroom window, sat out on the sill with her back to the street and struck out with a broom at an incendiary which had lodged in the gutter of her home. She managed, after a few wild shots, to hook it out and it fell into the street, where Patrick pounced on it happily and covered it with sand. Bridget eased herself back into her bedroom.

"Ow!" she exclaimed, as she caught her arm on a jagged piece of glass left in the window-frame. The blood gushing out looked black in the moonlight. Hastily she picked up her discarded apron from the bedroom chair and wrapped it tightly round the wound.

Early the next morning, a sympathetic Ellen Donnelly bathed off the apron stuck on the deep, ugly cut and rebandaged it tightly with a bit of an old pillowslip brought by Bridget. Afterwards, they finished the rest of Conor Donnelly's whiskey and, despite the pain, a fulminating Bridget went off to work in a large garage, where she spent her days sewing aeroplane canvas. As usual, her little boys went to school with clean hands and faces, and stomachs full of porridge.

About ten o'clock, an exhausted Conor arrived home. He was covered in dust from working on the results of a

47

direct hit on a dairy three streets away. "Three dead – and twelve cows spattered all over," he informed his sleepy wife. He went straight to the window and flicked back the half-drawn blackout curtains. "Where's me whiskey?"

"Me and Bridget Mahoney drank it," his wife said dully. "She were hurt." She was holding Michael to her breast and he was sucking eagerly. She did not look up.

In two strides her husband reached her. He struck her hard across her plump face. Then he stumbled upstairs to their bed and flung himself on to it.

ix

To alleviate the excruciating boredom of raidless nights, the clerks and shop assistants on fire guard duty in the buildings near the sailors' canteen would take it in turns to nip into the canteen for coffee. Mrs Robinson had once remarked that they complained when nothing happened and then they complained when there was a raid. "Then they're scared stiff, poor souls," she added.

Emmie had looked up at some of the steeply sloping roofs along which a firewatcher might have to clamber to get at a fire, and had been thankful that up to now the regular canteen staff had been excused from fire-watching.

Tonight, she entered the canteen through the narrow side passage which led into the light well at the rear. The light well was already shadowing and she fingered the long hat pin she kept under her coat lapel, until she had slipped through the kitchen door. You never knew who might be lurking at night in such a gloomy place as a light well, she told herself. A hat pin was a girl's best defence.

She greeted Doris, another paid member of the staff, who was shaking up a huge basket of potato chips above a vat of fat. Near her, with a bulging sack between them sat two volunteers patiently peeling and slicing further supplies for her. One lady dropped a handful of irregularly sliced chips into a bucket of water, and moaned, "This must be the most unromantic job in the whole war."

Emmie had lost some of her awe of these well-dressed ladies, and she teased them. "Now what would the boys out there do without chips? They couldn't go on without your chips. Proper miserable they'd be."

The volunteer nodded her head in rueful agreement and picked up another potato between her beautifully manicured nails. Then she chuckled. "You're quite right – they all seem to keep going on chips."

Emmie took her new lipstick from her handbag and clumsily outlined her lips in front of the kitchen mirror. She grimaced at the uncertain result. "Painted women are the devil's children," Gwen had told her. She smiled at herself in the mirror.

After years of having only Mrs Forster-Harrington to talk to, Emmie was happy in the company of the canteen staff. The customers were usually fun, too, she thought, though she did not always understand the jokes they made; and she was sure that to many she was only a pair of chapped hands bringing plates of food.

As she closed the wooden shutters over the big kitchen window looking out at the light well and then slotted the iron bar across them, she thought wistfully of Robert in his new ship. Perhaps after the war, when he could go back to being an inshore fisherman again, he could be at home more often, depending only on the time of the tides for his trips in and out.

She went to attend to a small window on the same wall. Carefully she drew a pair of old grey velvet curtains over it. Then she lifted the telephone off the table nearby and tucked it tightly against them, so that cracks of light would not show at the curtain hem. She had never in her life used a telephone and regarded it with some deference; Mrs Forster-Harrington had felt it unnecessary to have such an intrusion upon her privacy.

Despite the wail of the air raid siren, a steady buzz of conversation came through the thick tobacco smoke. Liverpudlians are not easily stopped in mid-argument, she reflected with a little smile. The men's aplomb lessened her own fear, and she bustled round her tables as if nothing unusual was happening outside.

In the kitchen, Doris stood clutching the edge of the pig bin in which all the kitchen scraps were kept for feeding pigs. She was trembling violently, her lined face as white as the tiles on the walls. She had lost home, husband and children in the Christmas air raids the previous year and the memory was still agonisedly fresh.

Lady Mentmore, a countess, lifted her beringed hands from the washing-up water and went to comfort her. Not by even the flicker of an eyelid did she show her own nervousness.

The gunfire was heavy and the quick thump-thump of bombs hastily discharged was unnervingly close. From a table in the corner near the kitchen door came the piercing sweet sound of a mouth organ. Almost

50

immediately a strong tenor voice joined in with the words, *She'll be comin' round the mountain when she comes*. There was a general roar of voices raised to sing what she would be wearing when she came, and Emmie tut-tutted to herself, as she dried dinner plates at record speed for the countess. What would Lady Mentmore think of such naughty words, worse than anything she had heard since she left school? Proper wicked little boys' words they were. Through the open door, she glimpsed the men's faces, red from exposure or yellow from too much confinement below decks. They glowed with pure mischief as they thought up new verses, each bawdier than the last. Doris gave the countess a watery smile and the countess unexpectedly chuckled.

The canteen closed at midnight, but most people there stayed on until the All Clear sounded about one o'clock. The volunteers murmured that they hoped all the ferry boats had not been sunk. "You can't walk on water," one laughingly remarked. Doris hoped the trams out to Bootle would still be running, and Emmie, who could walk home, hoped fervently that she would not be accosted by thieves, because she had just been paid. She transferred her pay packet from her handbag to her coat pocket and checked that her hat pin was still under her lapel; too many petty thieves, either singly or in small gangs, haunted the ill-lit streets and she was always nervous.

The light of the fires in the city made the shadows of the buildings still standing look even blacker than usual. She glanced at the sky. It was flushed in several directions and the smell of burning tobacco and smouldering rubber was thick in the air. Service vehicles of various kinds, with shaded headlamps, moved like dark ghosts. Except for two drunks helping each other along, there seemed to be no pedestrians. She began to run.

FRIDAY, 2nd MAY 1941

At half-past one on Friday morning, when Emmie let herself into her brother's house, an overwhelming smell of soot greeted her, but when she had lit a candle in the hallway, she was thankful to see that everything looked much as usual. She went straight upstairs, undressed and crept thankfully into bed.

At six o'clock the sound of Gwen's alarm jerked her awake, and she heard Mari next door clamber out of her creaky bed. Yawning, she crawled out herself, poured water from her ewer into a hand-basin on the wash-stand and splashed her face with it.

As she dried herself with a worn white towel, she whipped back the blackout curtains and saw a cheerful sun in a pale blue sky. Behind the houses across the back alley, the sky was flushed, but she argued hopefully to herself that it could be because the sun had not long risen. She hurried into an old cotton frock.

In the living room, the curtains were already drawn back, and David Thomas was kneeling on the hearth rug, clearing the ashes and soot from the hearth. "'allo, la," he greeted her amiably, between small, persistent coughs. "Proper mess, eh? Soon get t' fire goin', though."

Emmie agreed. Every stick of furniture was covered with a fine film of soot. It clung to the bronze Roman soldiers ornamenting each end of the high mantelpiece; it had coated the net curtains at the window and the fancywork runner across the middle of the table; even the four precious oranges in the fruit bowl on the sideboard were black. Gwen was going to be hard to live with today, she thought wryly.

David gave a sudden enormous sneeze and little puffs of soot rose round him.

Emmie clicked her tongue. "I'll get the floor cloth and wipe down the table and chairs, so as we can have brekkie," she said briskly. "Has the milk come?"

"I haven't looked."

Emmie went to the front door and peeped out. No milk bottle sat on the doorstep. "Well, I'm blowed," she exclaimed. "He's never missed before, not even in the Christmas blitz. I'll have to open a tin. Gwen's not going to like that."

Where the dairy once had stood, the milkman and his twelve cows lay neatly shovelled into bags, awaiting transport.

As she worked the tin-opener into a tiny tin of Nestle's milk, Emmie asked, "Did you have any incendiaries up here?"

"Aye. Had to put 'em out with sand. Woman who stores the stirrup-pump wouldn't open her door. Keeping the pump for herself, she was, in case her own house caught fire."

"That's proper awful."

"It was. I hope the warden gives her what for, today."

David, in clean overalls, was dispatched on time to the Royal Infirmary, where he was still repairing the plumbing damaged in the Christmas raids. A dreamy Mari was slapped by Gwen for not getting on with washing herself at the kitchen sink, scolded for not eating her cornflakes and was sent to school comparatively free of soot smudges.

With endless buckets of hot water and small amounts

of the irreplaceable, rationed soap, Emmie spent the morning washing down every nook and cranny of the living room and Gwen's bedroom, which was the only bedroom with a fireplace. The blackout curtains were taken into the back yard, put over the clothes-line and beaten, the net ones were washed and hung out to dry. The fireplaces were blackleaded and the oranges carefully scrubbed with a nail brush. Gwen herself sprinkled tea-leaves over the red, Belgian carpet in the sitting room and solicitously brushed it, remembering sadly the number of weeks it had taken her to pay for it, shilling by shilling. The china ornaments on the mantelpiece were lovingly bathed in the kitchen sink, the various messages printed on them in gilt twinkling *A present from Blackpool* or *Greetings from Llandudno* through the soapsuds. Gwen nearly cried. Lovely holidays those had been. She wondered when they would be able to go to the seaside again.

One of the whiting which Robert had caught made a consolingly large fish pie, some of which Gwen, Emmie and Mari ate at lunchtime. The rest was put away for David's tea.

Gwen reminded Emmie that she was due at Blackler's Store at one o'clock, to help in Dress Materials. She was very proud that she went to work two afternoons a week. Just before lunch, she changed into her best black dress, with its neat white lace collar, and her Sunday black stockings and shoes.

After she had left and Mari had returned to school, Emmie filled the kitchen bowl with hot water dipped from the oven tank beside the living room fire, stripped herself in the back kitchen and washed herself all over, in an effort to remove streaks of soot. Gwen did not encourage such scrubbings in the bedrooms – it made too many splashes on the polished linoleum.

ii

Next door, a sullen, resentful Ellen fried up some boiled potatoes and an egg and shoved them in front of her husband seated at the table. Conor was unusually quiet as he ate the food. When Ellen sat down by the fire, picked up 3-year-old Michael and gave him her breast, he stared past her, as if he were looking at something behind her.

The youngster suckled contentedly and Ellen enjoyed the physical pleasure of it, but finally her husband's oppressive silence became too much for her.

"What's to do with yez?" she asked sulkily.

He poked listlessly at his fried egg and sighed heavily. "It were a bad night, last night. The dairy were a shambles – blood everywhere – from the cows mostly. And them two women in Plum Street – bits of one of 'em hanging from the tree out front."

"Jesus Mary!" exclaimed Ellen. She shuddered, and Michael lost her nipple and complained fretfully. Her anger at Conor's striking her was forgotten in fascinated contemplation of this horror. She pushed her nipple back into Michael's mouth. "Maybe t' Nazis won't come again," she tried to comfort.

"There's nuthin' to stop 'em. 'specially at night. Play ducks and drakes they can." He contemplated a piece of grey potato on the end of his fork. "T' kid at the corner house 'as got a broken arm and bruises all over – part of the roof fell in on 'im. His dumb cluck of a mother left him in bed 'stead of bringing 'im down to the cellar."

"Poor little divil." She hugged her child closer and remembered, with a tremor, how close she had come to losing Ruby. What an evening that had been. The rest of the family had returned from a Christmas visit to the local cinema, to find the rescue men just hauling her out, unscratched, from under the kitchen table, which her grandfather had fashioned from oak fifty years before. She wondered idly if, when he had made it so solidly, he had had an intimation that it would save a life. Bless the sainted man. And God preserve her from another night like that.

iii

When Emmie descended from the tram, at her usual Church Street stop, on her way to work that afternoon, the traffic seemed nearly as busy as usual, though everywhere there was a strong smell of burning, and there was a general haze in the sky.

At the door of the canteen, she bumped into Doris, who promptly complained, "Me pore feet. Had to walk all the way to Bootle last night. Not a tram working. Bloody miles."

When Mrs Robinson and two volunteers arrived, they also looked tired after being up half the night, though all three were immaculately dressed. One of the volunteers, Mrs Starr, said, "I thought I was going to be late. We lost all our windows and I've been hammering old rugs over the downstairs ones ever since daybreak. First time I've ever used a hammer!"

Emmie listened to the lament. Did the stupid woman imagine that they had all been able to spend the morning in bed? In her opinion, complaining never did any good. You just took what life threw at you and did the best you could.

When the siren went, Emmie was busy serving a surge of men who had just come in after the closing of the public houses.

"Blow it," she exclaimed irritably, and some of the men made obscene gestures towards the ceiling. They were none of them drunk – publicans spread their meagre consignments of beer and spirits too thinly for anyone to achieve that happy state – but they were loquacious. Some of the language they used, as they consigned all Germans to Kingdom Come, made Emmie wonder innocently to Doris how Robert managed not to pick up such words.

Doris, trying to be brave, laughed shakily. "There never was a sea-going man what couldn't swear – your Robbie knows his manners, that's what it is."

While she doled out fish and chips – a little fish and a lot of chips – Emmie meditated on Doris's remark and realised that there was a side of her beloved which she did not know much about. For a minute or two, the sickening loneliness she had felt when her mother's coffin had been lowered into her grave was revived; and her new world of Robert Owen and the canteen seemed suddenly distant and alien.

As she cleared a table hastily evacuated by the buildings' firewatchers when they had fled back to their posts, there was a high-pitched swish-swish overhead.

Emmie froze. For a second all conversation stopped. The tiny silence was succeeded by a tremendous roar.

The room shook and the electric lights dipped. Everyone looked towards the ceiling.

A tumbling rumble announced the descent of the debris flung up by the explosion. Another roar, another series of rumbles.

Emmie stood terrified, the crockery rattling on her tray, as the guns began to answer the challenge of the planes.

"Put your tray down, luv, or you'll break everything." Deckie Dick, the friend of Robert's who had breakfasted with him on the morning he had first met Emmie, took the tray from her and put it back on the table. "Those two was away over ..." he began.

His voice was drowned by a crash that numbed her ears. His arms went round her and she was clamped against an old navy sweater that reeked of perspiration, as he sought to protect her face and head. In the kitchen, Doris screamed.

"Phew! That was near." Deckie Dick slowly let her go and she giggled nervously. As the guns continued their steady tattoo, a man at the next table chipped Dick, "You never misses a chance with the girls, do you?" Dick gave him a playful punch on the head, and Emmie slipped away to continue her clearing of tables.

Another crash, somewhere at the back of the building, brought Mrs Robinson running from the kitchen. "Gentlemen, there is a shelter downstairs. Take the staircase to the left of the front door. I think it would be a good idea ..." She was cut off by a series of appalling crashes, when again all faces automatically looked up at the ceiling. A crack zipped across it, but it held.

"Come on, lads. Everybody downstairs. Come on."

Deckie Dick began to move amongst the tables, touching men on their shoulders and pointing to the staircase. He turned to Mrs Robinson. "Get your ladies down, missus. It's going to be a bad night."

Without a word, she hastened back to the kitchen, where Doris was trying not to have hysterics in front of a pile of fish which she had been flouring. The fish was now covered with heavy dust.

Outside, fire engines raced pell-mell through the darkness, amid the shrill blare of burglar alarms set going in the shaken buildings opposite. Boots pounded past the front door, as rescue crews and air raid wardens ran by.

The customers no longer felt the need to look brave; the pandemonium outside was bad enough to justify a retreat, and they followed the volunteers down to the basement as fleetly as they would have abandoned a sinking vessel. Mrs Robinson, white-faced captain of her little ship, refused to descend until everyone was safely down. Then she quietly followed her crew.

At the foot of the stairs, she closed a very ancient, heavy door, bound with iron, hung there, presumably, to keep out eighteenth-century thieves and rioters. As she lowered the iron latch, she heard the upstairs front windows and shutters blow in, and the tinkle of slivers of glass sweeping across the canteen, to bury themselves in walls and tables. The blast reversed itself and blew outwards, causing a resounding crash of crockery from the tables. There was a muffled bang, when the shutters hit the empty window-frames again.

"Pooh!" she exclaimed. "Just in time." She sank down thankfully on one of the timeworn school benches which had been provided as seating.

The shelter was a windowless cellar, used for years for the storage of coal to heat the building. Its only entrance, other than the stairs, was a pavement light of heavy glass set in an iron frame. This could be swung upwards to facilitate the delivery of sacks of coal; in the construction of the shelter, it had been left as it was. A simple bolt on the inside held it down and it would form a convenient escape hatch from the basement to the street in the event of fire. Though the walls had been freshly whitewashed and the floor well swept, there was still a smell of coal. As a first line of defence against fire, a stirrup-pump with several buckets of water stood in a corner. In another corner was a small table; on it lay an electric ring and a clutter of much used tea-making apparatus. A single bulb hanging, unshaded, from the centre of the ceiling provided the only light.

Some of the men stood around smoking, while others slouched on the benches. Four of them sat cross-legged on the floor and prepared for a long wait by dealing out a pack of cards. The two volunteers sat primly together, backs straight; two middle-class women determined to be stoical.

A shivering Emmie sat by Doris with her arm round her. The bombed-out woman was sobbing quietly to herself, tears glistening on her rouged cheeks.

"Have a cigarette, me duck. It'll calm you."

A tall, thin seaman, a cigarette wobbling at the corner of his mouth, squatted down in front of Doris and generously proffered a precious packet of Player's. "You like one, luv?" he asked Emmie.

Doris smiled wanly, but made no move to take a cigarette. "Neither of us smoke," Emmie responded for both of them. "Ta, all the same."

The man turned back to Doris. "Well, you start. You're the woman that was bombed out, wasn't yez?"

Doris's eyes clenched shut. She nodded agreement.

"You should smoke. It helps. See, I'll show you how."

Her mind diverted, Doris opened her eyes. He was not a young man and bore all the marks of years of seagoing, of rotten food and working in cramped spaces. He grinned and lit a cigarette for her, drew the first breath on it and handed it to her. "There y'are, luv," he said, his sallow, hollow-cheeked face compassionate.

Emmie watched him wonderingly, captivated by his easy goodwill. Really, she thought, men *can* be kind; and she remembered, for a second, her father's unremitted bad temper. Who else, of the male sex, had she really known, other than him – and stolid, dull David? They had been no particular recommendation for their sex. She had taken Robert purely on trust; and how lucky she had been. The squatting seaman wondered why she suddenly smiled so sweetly.

While Doris cautiously puffed at her first cigarette, the barrage of noise persisted, as in steady waves the Luftwaffe swept over the doomed port. They were guided, at first, by the fires started the previous night and then by huge conflagrations which now began to flare in every direction. Far down the river, the flames' reflection danced on the water, lit up the rooms of suburban homes and warned ships at sea not to cross the bar. Forty miles away, in the Isle of Man, residents peeped between their bedroom curtains, to watch the blaze on the horizon mount higher and higher. "Liverpool's getting it again," they told each other in shocked whispers, so as not to wake the children.

In the shelter, two young deckhands who had drunk a

lot of beer decided that they must go to the lavatory. In a brief lull in the noise outside, they ran up the stairs, across the littered canteen, out through the kitchen door to the cobbled light well, where stood the ancient loos. As they relieved themselves, they look fearfully back over their shoulders through the open doors. What had once been, long ago before the offices had been built round it, the courtyard of a rich merchant's house now seemed to be a deadly funnel, down which bits of debris, shrapnel and occasional sparks travelled with unnerving rapidity. After a quick peek through the empty window facing the street, they were thankful to get back to the shelter.

"Proper shambles out front," one of them reported. "Beams and wires and stones scattered all over. Them last ones must've hit real close."

One of the card players looked up from his seat on the floor, pushed his plug of tobaco into one cheek and said, with a faint sneer, "Don't need a crystal ball to know they're close. Listen to 'em now."

"Ah, shut yer gob," retorted the returned youngster, hitching his braces up under his jacket.

"Now, gentlemen, this is no time to get upset," Mrs Robinson interjected hastily, having no illusions regarding the shortness of tempers amongst her usually overwrought, seagoing customers.

The young man made a wry face at Mrs Robinson and drifted over to the other side of the room, while the man on the floor muttered irritably, "Think they're bloody heroes every time they go to pee."

The second young man had kept his mouth shut, but now he said, with a tinge of wonderment in his voice, "There's a WVS canteen parked at the corner. T' women's doling out tea and sandwiches as if they was in their parlours at home. Feedin' the firemen, I think they are. Ordinary women just like me mam. And the flak flying round 'em like confetti."

A fast salvo of bombs nearly deafened them. Everybody crouched, hands over heads, fully expecting to be buried. When they found they had survived, they ruefully rubbed piercingly painful ears. From the ceiling, whitewash snowed gently.

Suddenly, all heads were raised; all noses sniffed. Smoke. The smell of burning wood was unmistakable. Fear jumped from one face to another. Some people rose quickly to their feet. Doris whimpered, and Emmie felt a rising panic.

"Hold it. No point in getting scared." Deckie Dick got up and put his pipe into his trouser pocket. "I'll nip upstairs and take a dekko for you. If I call, you come up orderly, mind."

The men quickly made a passage for him. Elderly, well-known and with forty years of seagoing experience spanning the First World War, he commanded respect. He ran swiftly up the stairs, the deck of cards which gave him his nickname bulging in his back trouser pocket.

The crowd relaxed slightly as, above the now more distant rumbles from outside, they could hear him working his way through the tumbled furniture of the canteen overhead. The back door slammed, indicating that it was still on its hinges.

Nothing was burning in the light well, though it was smoky. In the flickering light of fire reflected in the remaining windows of the offices across the street, he made his way to the front door with its protective sandbags. He flattened himself against the battered wall of sandbags, as a whistle sounded overhead. A huge explosion from South Castle Street sent shock waves running, and his ears rang. He listened, as intently as his hurt ears allowed. The throb of engines seemed to come from a greater distance, but in the street the smoke was thickening rapidly. Taking a big breath, he ran across the street and looked back up at the roof of the building housing the canteen. There was no sign of its being on fire, though it was outlined against a scarlet sky. The buildings on either side also showed no hint of fire.

He raced back across the road and down the steps again to the shelter. He reported, panting, "T' smoke's nothing, as far as we're concerned," and then paused to get his breath while another series of detonations drowned him out. Emmie felt her courage draining from her and she and Doris clung to each other. He continued, "There's some big fires not far away – and I could hear machine guns for a minute. Bloody Boche going for the firemen." He looked at the anxious faces surrounding him. "If we try to move, like as not we'll walk into more trouble. I'd say stay here." He sat down suddenly on a bench, aware that he was no longer as young as he had been. He looked down at his shabby boots, while men slowly resumed their seats.

When his heart had stopped racing, he said diffidently, "Think I'll walk up Lord Street and see what's to do. T' rescue squads must be hard-pressed at the back there. Anybody want to come?"

The men stopped their subdued gossiping and looked uneasily at Dick, and Dick said, "Them as has wives and kids, maybe you shouldn't. A couple of you is perhaps like me – you can please yourselves."

"My family is killed in Antwerp," said a melancholy Dutch voice from the far end of the room. "Who to rescue? This is shops and offices round here. Nobody here." He got up, a big, handsome blond man towering over most of those present.

"There's firewatchers and caretakers in every building," replied Dick simply. "Young girls, some of them watchers is."

Two men in naval uniform stood up and the four of them, without a further word, eased their way through to the staircase. Not to be outdone by the Royal Navy, two merchant seamen followed them.

Mrs Robinson said brightly, "As soon as the raid is over, we'll see if we can clean the canteen up, ready for business tomorrow."

The women nodded tired agreement. Emmie was stiff with fatigue and the enforced idleness; the worst thing about air raids was, she thought, that you couldn't hit back.

The electric light went out. Emmie gave a frightened squeak and Doris drew in her breath quickly. The glowing ends of lighted cigarettes looked like red eyes staring in the darkness. A man laughed shakily. A voice from the gloom said bitterly, "If that isn't the bottom!"

There was a jingle of keys and change, as Mrs Robinson rummaged in the depths of her shabby crocodile-skin handbag. "I've got a match somewhere. There should be some candles in the drawer of the table."

Someone lit a match and a male voice from near the floor said, "I've got a torch, Missus."

The beam seemed as brilliant as a searchlight.

"Oh, thank you," she cried, stumbling over feet as, guided by the torch, she went to the table. She snapped the drawer open. "Really!" she exclaimed. "This is too bad. Somebody has stolen both the candles and the matches. There's not even a stump here."

There was an angry murmur through the room. Petty theft was a way of life in Liverpool. Now, with everything in short supply, it could cause real problems. The owner of the torch, however, said magnanimously, "Anybody as needs to move, tell me and I put me torch on."

Batteries were harder to obtain than candles, so when a young voice said, "Thanks, friend," it expressed the feelings of everybody.

Listening to the clamour outside, while sitting in total darkness was far worse, thought Emmie. The minutes seemed longer; the noise wrapped one closer. People tended not to talk; instead they huddled together for comfort.

Gwen had told her of a woman in the next street, who had clung to a perfect stranger in the street's unlighted shelter, while they sat out the Christmas Eve raid, the year before. In their terrible fear, they had become sexually aroused, and now she was pregnant by a man she had never seen. Shocking, Gwen called it; but David, with unexpected understanding, had said that it was Mother Nature's way of seeing that people who had died in a disaster were replaced.

Gwen had responded tartly, "More likely they didn't know right from wrong."

As she hugged Doris, Emmie wondered if she herself were pregnant, or whether the change of life was making its presence felt. Though frightened, in her secret heart she hoped that she was still young enough for a bun to be in the oven, Robert's little one.

"I hope Robbie's sailed and out of this rumpus," she whispered to Doris.

"You might get a letter tomorrer," Doris suggested. Her own heart ached at the thought; even the letters her dead husband had written to her when they were courting had been lost, with him, in their burned-out home.

The racket outside seemed to be slackening, the explosions further away. "Sounds like they might be doin' Bootle or Seaforth," suggested a disembodied voice.

"God spare us," exploded Doris. "Haven't we had enough up there?"

iv

The women stood forlornly at the top of the shelter stairs. The All-Clear had sounded; the noise abated. Through the gaping front windows, the whole town seemed to glow, the shattered room lighted up as if a good coal fire was burning in the old-fashioned grate. As they moved forward, glass and china crunched beneath their feet. The counter, which normally held the tea and coffee samovars, flanked by plates of buns and sandwiches, had been swept clear. Both samovars lay on their sides on the floor, silent humps in pools of black liquid, their copper exteriors reflecting the dancing light from outside.

The light from outside did not penetrate the kitchen,

so Mrs Starr struck a match. "Ah, that's better," she cried.

Though very dusty, the kitchen was practically undisturbed. The telephone, which Emmie had put on the sill to hold down the blackout curtains of the small window, had fallen on to the table beneath the window. Emmie lifted the curtain to peer out and was surprised that, at least there, there was still glass to look through.

Mrs Starr, one of the volunteers, asked Mrs Robinson a little diffidently, "Would you mind if I phoned my son to say I am all right?"

Mrs Robinson looked up from her task of setting out candles and lighting them. "Of course not," she replied.

The phone was dead. Mrs Starr sighed, and looked at her watch. It was nearly 3 a.m.

An air raid warden paused by the open front door. "Anybody here?" he shouted. Drawn by the sudden flare of the candles, he clumped towards the kitchen. His face was gaunt, eyes burning with fatigue. A striped pyjama collar stuck out untidily from the neck of his uniform.

"Are we safe from the fires?" Mrs Robinson asked, after greeting him.

"Aye. There's a firewatcher on the roof – young Dolly – she'll tell you if fires out t' back are spreading this side."

"What's burning?" Mrs Starr asked.

"Church House. It'll be gutted. Too far gone to save. And the Corn Exchange and the White Star building – God knows how many others. Bootle's calling for fire-engines out there, but they can't spare none from here." He heaved a sigh. "Must go check next door. Ta-ra." He crunched his way back across the strewn

71

canteen floor and they heard him curse as he caught his boot against one of the recumbent samovars and it clanged like a bell.

While Emmie and Gwen cleaned up their home and David laid new waterpipes in the Royal Infirmary, Conor walked round his district to assess the damage of the previous night.

"Rain'll do more damage than t'bombs," he told the already very depressed families, who a few streets away from his own home had lost their roofs. "I'll get you some tarps to lay over the rafters."

He returned to the post and put in a request for tarpaulin. Then he retrieved the front and back doors of the oldest couple affected, and helped the old man hang them again.

From nearby homes still comparatively undamaged, older women, silent, hands clasped over their stomachs, drifted over to watch and then to help their stricken neighbours shovel plaster and soot out of their chaotic little homes. Children, too small for school, found jam butties thrust into their hands by strange, smiling women. Buckets of water and trays of tea were lugged from several streets away, where water was still available. Friendships which were to last a lifetime were made between tearful outbursts from women beginning to quiver from delayed shock. The acute shortage of young, strong men to help was remarked upon and an extra tear was shed for those of them fighting in Greece or on a warship somewhere in the

Mediterranean. And slowly, painfully slowly, some order was restored.

While he munched a very dry sandwich, back at the post, Conor wrote out his reports. After that, seething with rage, he went to see the bitch who had refused to produce the street's stirrup-pump, at a time when the whole road had been littered with incendiaries.

God, how he needed a drink. He seemed to be floating, rather than walking. Lightheaded, that was the word. And what a fool he had been to put at the back of the cellar of the post the half dozen bottles of whiskey he had lifted from a lorry unwise enough to park in the district a couple of days before. Now, the post was as busy as a tram terminus and he could not retrieve them without its being noticed. If he had found a better place for them, he could have had a drink right now and flogged the rest for good money.

He slammed down his fountain pen and went home.

With one side of her face still slightly swollen from the blow he had given her, Ellen was in no mood to be conciliatory. Practically the whole of the family's bacon ration piled on his plate, however, suggested that the storm might be passing. He was too tired, too overwhelmed by other people's troubles laid upon his shoulders, to make an effort to break the silence between them, and as soon as he had mopped up the last bit of grease from his plate with a piece of bread, he announced that he was going to bed.

Within minutes, he was sound asleep, and did not hear Ellen shouting exasperatedly at Patrick's back, as he went out of the front door.

"I'm not going to bed at seven o'clock, no matter how many raids there are," he had said obstinately. "I'm goin' to see a pal." And he had wandered out into the deserted street, with a lazy grin at her over his shoulder.

He slipped through the soft spring evening, to the unfinished, roofless air raid shelter where he had taken Mari and where she had reluctantly promised to meet him again. He hung around outside it for nearly an hour, but Mari did not come.

A thoroughly scared Mari was certain that the previous night's raid had been arranged by God particularly to punish her.

He walked back home, clenched fists in trouser pockets, shoulders hunched, muttering angrily under his breath. Nothing but a stuck-up Judy, that's her. Wait till he caught her again. Yet, beneath his rage, he felt no true desire to harm her; only a craven fear that she would not come again; a young Romeo who had not yet managed to persuade his Juliet to fall in love with him. Wait till he was a Spitfire pilot, he reassured himself, with embroidered wings on his tunic; then she'd come crawling, and he might just condescend to take her to a dance.

At half-past ten, he was sitting despondently on the basement steps, listening to the guns and whistling to himself, while a fearful Ruby crouched close to him, pulling nervously at her thick, black fringe. Their sleepy father had tumbled back into his overalls and gone down to the post.

vi

Dress Materials at Blackler's had, that Friday afternoon, been busy. Women were buying dress lengths, in anticipation of clothes being rationed; Gwen herself had several such lengths stored away in the mahogany chest of drawers brought from Emmie's home. Out of her wages, she was also holding a little money in order to buy two pairs of silk stockings, which a girl from Hosiery had told her, during her tea break, had at last arrived.

She was surprised when her supervisor sent her over to the Dress Department to help out.

"They're rushed off their feet," she explained. "People wanting mourning clothes."

When, homeward bound, she descended from the tram at the corner of her street, her feet ached abominably. She had sold so many black dresses that she felt deeply dispirited. At one point, she had been positively thankful to be faced with a giggling 15-year-old who wanted a pale blue bridesmaid's dress.

"Me sister's boy friend's got a forty-eight-hour pass. Comin 'ome Tuesday night. Me mam's nearly out of her mind tryin' to get everything ready for a wedding on Wednesday mornin'." The girl's flippant elation had made several sad-faced women turn on her with reproving murmurs of "Really! At this time?" Unable to relate to the grief of strangers, she had gone away happy, with a fluff of blue net carefully packed in tissue paper.

"Phew!" Gwen groaned, as she tottered through the twilight. The sky was still an unnaturally bright pink, but she was too tired to care. She thought only of her clean bed, with David, solid and reliable, snoring on his side of it.

"Where's your dad?" she asked Mari, as she took off her Sunday hat, black velveteen with a bunch of feathers

75

held by a *diamanté* brooch, and laid it carefully in its box.

The girl lifted a wan face from gloomy contemplation of her arithmetic book and wiped her pen nib with a piece of blotting paper. "I don't know, Mum. I'm scared. It's late for him."

"Ach, he's probably doin' overtime. What did you do with his bit of fish pie?"

"I kept it hot for a while. Then it got so dried out in the oven, I put it back in the pantry."

"Good girl."

Good girl? Mari chewed the end of her plait nervously, and sighed, and tried to forget the extraordinary sensations within her.

About midnight, David staggered in and thankfully plunked down his heavy tool-box.

"Worked late and then I had to walk home," he told them as, regardless of the guns roaring outside, they scuttled round to get him his supper. "There's a proper raid on down town. The sound of the planes diving, as I come along, give me the willies, they did. Hope our Em's all right."

Gwen had forgotten entirely about Emmie and now she paused, tea caddy in hand, a twinge of conscience striking her.

"Anyway, we can't do anything about her," he went on practically, as he sat down to his fish pie. "We should go to bed. They're not bombing round here — too busy with the town to bother us." He turned to Mari and said with a grin, "Your room's a deal safer with the window being boarded up. Maybe young Patrick did you a good turn."

Mari stared at him for a second, her smile frozen on

her face. Then she said diffidently, "I suppose he did."

Gwen climbed nervously into her bed and pulled the clothes over her head, to shut out the sound of chugging aeroplane engines. Two hours of sitting on the basement steps had made her back ache and to lie down was a blessed relief. David put his head on his pillow and began to snore immediately. Mari lay quietly in the stuffy darkness of her room and wondered what had really happened to her. Could you have a baby if a boy touched you?

None of them heard Emmie's flagging footsteps, when she came in. Groaning sleepily, they got up again at six o'clock in the morning and were astonished to find her sound asleep in David's chair, a cold cup of tea beside her on the bookshelf.

SATURDAY, 3 MAY 1941

Gwen stared unbelievingly at the shattered windows of Blackler's store. She seethed with indignation. An attack on Blackler's was, she felt, an attack on her personally. It was *her* store.

She glanced along its usually immaculate frontage. Little piles of swept-up glass stood waiting to be shovelled away. The gaping holes which had once been windows filled with merchandise labelled with large, cheerful notices of special bargains, had been cleared; only one or two, where the glass, by some fluke, remained intact, still bravely displayed for the benefit of the weekend invasion of shoppers from Wales a collection of special offers.

And the Welsh were coming in in force. Dressed in their best, they came by train and bus not only to buy but to make holiday, joining shoppers from the Liverpool suburbs, in touring the damage wreaked on the city and viewing the roaring fires. People from slum and suburb alike walked into cafés and grocery shops whose fronts had been blown out, and stood around feasting on food not yet salvaged. Rowdy groups, dodging the already harassed police, calmly looted anything they fancied, laughing and joking and getting drunk on wines and spirits they found in the grocery stores. Not a few owners defended their little broken shops with cricket bats, battered symbols of integrity.

As, later on, she snipped lengths of material for a customer who spoke, with disgust, of the behaviour of a group of hooligans she had seen, Gwen said bitterly,

"You'd think we was a circus, the way they gape – and a free-for-all. Rob their own mothers, they would."

"Aye," the customer agreed heavily. "Who'd have believed it?"

ii

David usually finished work at twelve noon on Saturdays, and Gwen had left a dish of stew in the oven for his midday meal. It grew dryer and dryer and finally shrivelled up on the plate, because David had not, that morning, been pursuing the incredible intricacies of the plumbing of the Royal Infirmary. He had, instead, been pounced on by his supervisor, immediately upon his arrival, and had been sent by taxi out to Bootle, together with his mate, Arthur, a grizzled ancient, back in the work force after four years of retirement.

"Bloody chaos out there," the supervisor had told them. "No water. Gas lines flaring up in the streets. Electric's out. Report to the town hall. They'll tell you where to go."

They were joined by two electricians, who had also been impounded, and as they sat in the taxi, tool-boxes rattling in the luggage compartment by the driver, they looked out in astonishment and no little trepidation at increasing turmoil, the further north they proceeded.

The driver had to pick his way through miles of littered streets made muddy by burst water lines and, in places, lacings of fire-hoses temporarily abandoned for lack of water pressure. Timber yards crackled and smoked on both sides of the road, the draught of the flames making it hard for the driver to keep the taxi stable, for a scarifying few minutes. Occasionally, they would be redirected by police or special constables, to detour a mass of masonry spread across a street.

When they finally found the streets they were to work in, after being redirected by a series of city officials, they stood for a moment bewildered, their tools at their feet, wondering where in earth to start. Civil defence workers of every kind toiled amid the havoc, while the homeless scrambled over the debris in an effort to pick out some belongings which might still be usable. In desperate efforts to help families still entombed, some of them got into the way of rescue workers cautiously digging through piles of bricks, mortar and shattered wood, to get at victims for whom there was little hope. Others stood in forlorn groups, an occasional sob indicating some poor soul for whom it was all too much; still others were unnaturally cheerful, thankful to have survived; the true hardship of their situation would hit them later.

A hundred yards up the street, a cracked gas line gave way. A white sheet of flame roared upwards, its deadly heat threatening further damage. Rescuers and inhabitants scrambled over debris to a safer distance.

"Good God!" exclaimed Arthur, and turned to run.

David caught his arm. His breath came in frightened gasps, but he said, "It could blow the whole street up. Better find the valve. See if we can turn it off." He grabbed a tool from his box and followed by a protesting Arthur ran towards the explosion. While wardens shouted to them to come back, they searched likely spots for the valve they needed, and, within a minute or two, found it. A quick twist and the flame subsided. David stood very still for a moment, holding on to Arthur, while the pain in his chest subsided, a shivering unsung hero, like many others that day.

Soon, watched anxiously by housewives, black-shawled against the morning coolness, David and Arthur were set to work by a city hall official to reconnect a major break in a water line. The women were desperate for water to clean their damaged homes and wash the dirt off their children and themselves. The Women's Voluntary Service brought food both to workers and watchers, and they stood around in the street, their children about them, while they thankfully sipped mugs of tea. Their voices were shrill with nervous tension and they wound their shawls tightly round themselves for comfort. To David, it seemed particularly wicked that people so painfully poverty-stricken should have their tiny, crowded homes broken open like eggs. "And the men at sea – or struggling to keep the docks working," David muttered angrily to Arthur.

There was no question of going home that night; the need of them in Bootle was too grave.

As twilight approached, he and Arthur paused to stretch themselves and eat the sandwiches brought to them by the indefatigable WVS canteen staff. They both became aware of a general movement in the neighbourhood. Women, pushing perambulators or pushchairs loaded with children and bedding, were so numerous as to form a long procession in the now partially tidied up street.

"Where do you think they're goin'?" he asked Arthur.

"Walkin' out to Huyton, to sleep in t' fields, I expect. It's a deal safer'n staying here overnight."

David nodded. Except for an occasional shout to a child to mind himself, the procession was strangely quiet. There was a dull acceptance in the passing faces, framed in dusty, tousled hair. Dragging boots made a slow shuffling sound on the gritty street.

"They'll be back in t' mornin', bright and early no doubt," remarked Arthur, "to check on their homes – and sent t' kids to school – if the school's still there."

iii

Mari and her friend, Dorothy, went to the Saturday, children's programme at the cinema that afternoon and then went home to Dorothy's house for tea.

While his mother sat on the front step, nursing Michael and enjoying the sunshine, and Ruby and Nora played skipping on the pavement, Patrick sloped around the alleyways, hoping to find Mari. Unsuccessful, he irritably teased his father's fighting cocks and for his pains got a long scratch on the back of his right hand.

Conor Donnelly's area had been mercifully free from incidents on the previous night, so while he had a comparatively quiet day, he wandered down to the Hercy Dock to see if he could find an American sailor off a tanker, with nylons or lipsticks for sale. Both fetched good prices on the black market.

iv

As Gwen bustled into her home about eight o'clock that evening, she felt more energetic than she had done for some days. A few hours of good sleep, despite the noise of the raid, had restored her, and she had enjoyed at Blackler's the close feeling of unity amongst her companions, engendered by their joint dislike of the large influx of sightseers and ill-intentioned riff-raff into the town.

Mari was sitting alone, by the fire, slowly turning the heel of a sock, one of a pair she was knitting as a contribution to a parcel being made up for the men of the King's Regiment. Two of the girls in the class had fathers serving in it, stationed at Hull. Mari was a good knitter, having been taught by her mother as soon as she could hold a pair of butcher's skewers and a ball of wool.

"Yer dad not in?" Gwen inquired, as she once more returned her best hat to its box.

"No." Mari paused, needle in stitch.

Mari was feeling a little less panic-stricken about Patrick. She had stuck close to Dorothy all day, and after tea they had rearranged Dorothy's doll's house and put up new curtains in it. Mr Hale, Dorothy's father, who had to go to a chapel meeting, had kindly walked her home, since it was on his way. They walked slowly because he limped; Dorothy said he had been wounded in the First World War at a terrible place called Passchendaele, and, as had sometimes happened in her grandfather's house, Mari was reminded that the results of war stayed on and on, long after the battles were finished. Did it mean, she wondered fearfully, that her life would be different after the war? Would she, all her life, drag a foot or, much worse, be jeered at because she had been disfigured? She nearly choked, when she remembered that her grandfather had once told her that he had a friend kept permanently in hospital because he had almost no face.

She had thought about this, as she sat quietly knitting; it was all mixed up with a hodge-podge of ideas about Patrick. To her relief, her figure had not swelled up as she knew a pregnant woman's did, so she had begun to think that being caressed all over by a boy's exploring fingers did not produce a baby, and that was a relief; she had heard of girls who had committed suicide because they were pregnant and did not have a proper husband.

The explosive feelings that Patrick had aroused in her must mean something, though. She longed to ask her mother about it, but dared not. Could such an exciting feeling really be wicked? She wondered if she could ask Aunt Emmie; after all, she was engaged and must know something about it.

As Gwen put the kettle on for tea, she was not particularly worried about David; he had done a lot of overtime recently. Both mother and daughter jumped apprehensively, however, when someone thumped on the front door.

"Your dad? Hurt?" Gwen exclaimed.

As they ran along the passage, getting in each other's way in their sudden sense of urgency, they heard Conor Donnelly outside, shouting, "Mrs Thomas! Mrs Thomas!" Gwen reckoned that if the warden brought the news, it must be bad. She flung the door open, letting out a little light from the candle on the hall table.

"Get in, get in," Conor ordered testily. "Enough light to guide them from Berlin."

He hastened over the doorstep and shut the door behind him.

"What's to do?" Gwen asked anxiously, while Mari's blank little face went whiter than usual.

"Och, it's all right," he answered, seeing their frightened faces. "Yer husband rang the post, from Bootle, to say he mayn't be back till tomorrer night."

"What? Bootle? What's he doin' there?"

"It's terrible out there, missus. They need every man they can get."

"How'll he get his dinner?"

"Same as the firemen and everyone else workin' out there. From the WVS canteen, I 'spect."

"He's too old to be gallivanting round out there. He needs his sleep." Gwen's voice was angry.

Conor's deep blue eyes registered such scorn that Gwen quailed slightly. "So do we all. We're none of us youngsters, Mrs Thomas."

She was disconcerted at the snub, and her irritation at this man and his slovenly family increased. She said tightly, "Well, thank you for bringing the message. I don't know why he didn't phone earlier."

"Phones out of order, like everything else," he replied, fully aware of her distaste of him.

Gwen went slowly back to the living room and sat down on a footstool close to the fire. It was wasteful to have a fire in May, but she justified it by cooking on it, and now, suddenly, she was grateful for its comforting warmth. For the first time in her life, the idea that she might be widowed occurred to her; Conor's description of the dire straits of Bootle had struck home; accidents happened in such awful situations.

While Mari made tea and toast for their supper, the virtues of her patient lumbering husband surfaced in her mind. She remembered, with a pang, the sturdy Welsh youth who had proposed to her, as they walked soberly in Princes Park after chapel. They had had to wait seven

88

years before they could afford to be married, and, sipping tea beside the fire, she wished they had not wasted their youth. Why, she wondered bitterly, had she been so coldly virtuous? And now it could all end in a holocaust in Bootle.

She and Mari had lain in bed a scant hour, when the air raid warning dragged them out again. "We'll get dressed in the living room," Gwen said resignedly. "It'll be safer down there."

"Poor Aunt Emmie," Mari exclaimed. "Stuck down town again."

v

Ellen Donnelly blasted furiously all them Jerries and their ilk, as she, too, that Saturday night shepherded her family down the cellar steps.

During the day, she had hauled a mattress down into the dank basement and on this she persuaded Ruby, Nora and Brendy to lie down to sleep. It was not quite so safe as sitting on the stairs, but as she remarked, "Beggars can't be choosers."

Patrick sat moodily on the top step, watching his mother nurse Michael to sleep again. The candlelight caught the white hairs amongst her brown mop and deepened the lines on her shiny red face. He felt a sudden twinge of pain that his mother was growing older. Though she was always demanding to know where he had been and what he had been doing, he loved her with a passion that frightened him sometimes. He was inordinately jealous of his father, and, when his father struck her, he boiled with inward anger that he was too small and cowardly to defend her. When I'm bigger, I will, he always told himself. He resented the succession of babies that occupied her lap, and only Ruby, eleven months younger than him, escaped being bullied by him whenever he was in a bad temper.

The noise of the anti-aircraft guns began to shake the old house.

vi

Unaware of the frantic clean-up done by candlelight after the previous night's raid, a dozen men were lounging round the tables of the sailors' canteen, gossiping amid the usual cloud of tobacco smoke.

Mrs Robinson arrived at the same time as Emmie. She was carrying two parcels and Emmie took them from her. "These are heavy," she exclaimed.

"Crockery oddments, my dear. After last night, we're dreadfully short. These are a donation from Lewis's – I went in to see them this morning."

In the kitchen, Peggie Evans, another paid member of the staff, was tidying up the last of the muddle from the lunchtime rush. "'T' fish is finished," she told Emmie and Mrs Robinson, "'T' butcher brought plenty of sausage, though, for tonight. And there's still a lot o' dried egg."

As she put on her overall, Emmie told her how the fish had been covered with dust the previous night. "At first we was goin' to throw it out. Then Mrs Robinson said what waste. So we washed it very carefully and put it in the larder. Did you have any complaints?"

"Never a word. Deep fried, there'd be nought the matter with it." She took her coat off a hook and her handbag out of a drawer. "Was I ever glad I wasn't here last night. It must've been awful."

"I were scared out of me wits," admitted Emmie. "I got a proper laugh, though, out of the note you've pinned on the sandbags round the door. 'Open for business – very open.'"

"Aye. I thought t' lads 'd believe we'd given up on 'em, with the shutters closed, like."

"You know we had the till cleaned out, during the raid?"

"No?"

"Somebody took the whole night's takings. Must've done it while we was in the shelter. We didn't stop to lock the front door."

"Stinking buggers," said Peggie forcefully, as she clapped a blue beret on her head. "Tara-well."

Doris did not arrive. She lay dead in the arms of the seaman who had taught her to smoke, under the wreckage of a shop doorway which had suddenly collapsed on them, taking both their lives while they made love.

A white-haired grocer's wife, Mrs Atkins, and the silent, elegant Lady Mentmore were redeployed to cover the work. "Perhaps she'll phone later," suggested Emmie.

"Is the phone working?" Mrs Robinson looked harried. She was bone-tired, her plump, middle-aged body refusing to run at its usual pace.

Emmie went to the table by the window and cautiously lifted the receiver and put it to her ear. "It's still dead," she announced.

"Oh, dear! What a nuisance! The crater down the street must be responsible for that. I saw the Post

91

Office Telephones van there, as I came in."

Mrs Atkins looked up from her carrot scraping. "It really was an awful night. And it could have been worse. I heard this morning that they were worried about a munition ship called the *Malakand* in Huskisson Dock. It's being loaded for the Middle East. And with the fires and that being so bad up the north end – poor Bootle – they were mortally afraid it would explode."

Emmie froze, the fork with which she was pricking sausages poised to stab. "The *Malakand*?" she exclaimed in horror. "My Robbie's on that." She turned a stricken face towards the carrot scraper. "He never told me it had munitions in it."

Mrs Atkins soothed, "Well, nothing's happened to it yet. Perhaps it will sail today."

Emmie nodded assent and slowly and heavily she pricked the neat pink rows of sausages. She tried not to weep. To sail the Med with ammunition in the hold! Even if he got out of port safely, it could be a death-warrant! She wanted to scream 'No' to God. Was He really almighty? She wanted to faint, to escape the fear which pierced her. But she could not, must not. In a war, she must not give way. Quietly, she went on with her work and missed the pitying glances of Mrs Atkins and the countess. The countess said practically, to Emmie's back, "I think we all need a cup of tea."

As she filled the four cups from the samovar, she herself was not feeling very well. The previous night, an incendiary, apparently a dud, had fallen through the thatched roof of her house, and it had taken the combined efforts of her two elderly maids and herself to lift it out of the water tank into which it had fallen. They had thrown it out of the attic window on to the lawn, where it had unexpectedly exploded. A small incident, not worth mentioning, but it had tired her. She yawned behind a heavily beringed hand, as she added lots of sugar to Emmie's tea; she understood that the lower classes enjoyed plenty of sugar.

vii

Saturday night, when you should be down at the local, sitting by the fire and telling funny stories over a pint of bitter; instead you were stuck in a sandbagged shop labelled A.R.P., listening to the pandemonium in the skies and hoping that nothing fell on you. The strain was telling on Conor Donnelly. He told himself irritably that he had had it up to here. And to add to it all, he had quarrelled with Ellen over a drop of whiskey – and she was still as sour as yesterday's milk. He went to the door and glanced up at the sky.

The brilliance of the flares had put the stars out, and the air smelled as if a million rubber tyres were burning. The shriek of bombs descending on the flaming city centre, about a mile down the hill, could hardly be heard above the concerted roar of their impact, the drone of heavy engines and the scream of night fighters as they dived. Nearer, in the park, the anti-aircraft guns kept up a steady barrage at the bellies of the bombers, which glistened like slugs, in the light of darting flames.

Inside the post, three women wardens were placidly waiting for a tin kettle of water to boil on a primus stove, their imperturbability belied by their ghostly faces. A grey-haired voluntary warden, Montagu Smith, who came in each night there was a raid, was snatching

93

a nap on a camp-bed. In the daytime, he was the manager of the bank round the corner.

Conor had always thought that anyone who had a bank account, never mind worked in a bank, must be hopelessly stuck up. But this pot-bellied man had won his admiration the previous November. He had crawled into the shifting debris of a house, to hold the hand of a dreadfully injured old man until a doctor crawled in, too, to give the victim an injection to ease the pain while they got him out. Then they had worked the remainder of the night together, under enemy machine-gun fire.

The half-washed Irish labourer and the well-shaven polite banker supported each other. Conor never gave himself credit for the friendliness he exuded, the enthusiasm with which he would do a good turn. Montague – our Mont, to all the wardens – had a quick, orderly mind, able to size up the immediate needs in some of the horrid situations which they faced together.

"G' us a cuppa tea, Glynis, luv," Conor asked one of the women. He was hungry. In a day or two, Ellen would get over her sulks and boil up a good stew. Meanwhile, he could whistle for it. A short burst of machine-gun fire directly overhead made everyone duck instinctively. He wished suddenly he had made it up with Ellen. What was a drop of whiskey anyway, in a world where one bullet could finish him? He chewed his thumb uneasily while Glynis made the tea.

Glynis Hughes eased her tin hat further back on her head and grinned up at him. She was a small, brown-skinned woman, suggesting descent from the little people who roamed Britain before the Celts arrived. Her husband was serving in the South Lancashires and she was temporarily living nearby with her mother. She worked in a factory which made aircraft parts and she made many a lewd joke about her production of joysticks. She was used to coping with the appetite of a labourer in a steelworks and she still shamelessly bought any food she could find on the black market. Now she asked, "Like a Spam sandwich?"

"Ah would, if you can spare it."

She took out from a shopping bag a white, confectioner's paper bag and from this she carefully drew out a sandwich two inches thick with a thin slice of Spam in it. "I brought some bikkies for you girls," she told her companions, "Chocky ones."

The other two women's faces lit up. "Mm. Where did you get them from?" They, too, were housewives permanently scrounging through the shops for extra food. To earn the money for it, they worked as labourers, cleaning oil drums at a petrol installation.

Glynis giggled. "Ask no questions, you'll be told no lies."

Conor wolfed the proffered sandwich and a chocolate biscuit. He felt much better and walked outside to take another look at what was happening.

The sky was a brilliant pink, with rolling billows of smoke making rosy cushions above him. There was no one, not even a cat, in the street. He went back into the tiny shop and leaned against the wall by the telephone girl, to gossip.

He was jolted upright by a fast puffing sound, closer than the general roar, then a pause, while everyone held their breath. A heavy crump and everyone breathed out.

"Land-mine," Conor said. "Unexploded."

"Must have fallen in the park," Glynis commented, relief exuding from her.

"Here comes another," squeaked the telephonist, as she laid her head on her table and clasped her arms over her tin hat. The trainlike sound came again and Conor tensed.

An enormous explosion shook the old shop, reverberating round them in swelling waves. The telephone girl was nearly lifted off her chair, and cracks ran up the grubby walls. Mont was on his feet in a split second, clapping his helmet to his head. "My God!" he exclaimed.

A colossal growl, like that of some huge animal, indicated the fall of heavy masonry; it was followed by a rapid tattoo of smaller pieces on to the roof and into the street.

"The tenement?" breathed Glynis through chattering teeth. "The Dwellings?"

"Could be," Mont replied, as he loosened his torch from his belt. All of them dreaded a direct hit on the huge five-storey tenement nearby. It was built in a circle, round a communal yard, and was packed with young families.

Conor had already gone. He ran madly down the pink-lit street and turned left. He was brought up short by an impenetrable cloud of dust. Other than the heavy grumble from the skies, there was a weird silence.

Then, from beyond the dust cloud, came scream after scream of pain and panic. "Oh, Jesus, help us," shrieked a woman's voice.

Doors of the row houses close to the warden banged open, as shaken tenants came rushing out. Mont panted up to Conor, and said, "I'll tell Josie to phone R. and P. We're going to need a lot of help."

Conor cleared his throat and spat. "Better have a

96

closer look first. Could be only the houses facin', not the tenement itself."

They both took out handkerchiefs to cover their noses from the cloying dust; it was so thick that the beams of their torches were reflected back, as if they faced a wall. They turned the lights down to their feet and picked their way round huge slabs of concrete and piles of bricks, interspersed with threatening electric wires. The dust, now mixed with a strong smell of gas, made Mont cough. He tripped over a broken beam and fell, barking his shins and hands painfully, and got up again. Behind him, Conor could hear other people scrambling over the wreckage; they were shouting to each other, as they converged, and above and beyond the sound of their voices came the screams of the half-crushed.

"'Allo, la," Conor called. "I'm the warden. All men come to me." Dear God, send me some wi' a bit o' savvy, he added to himself. Judging by the curses behind him, he was not going to have to *ask* people to help tonight, which was a welcome change. He hoped Tom Massey was on duty – biggest bloody rozzer in the whole police force. He knew he could use a dozen heavyweights for this job.

A shrieking woman blundered into him. She clutched his arms and shook him. "Me lads – me lads!" she yelled into his face. She was naked, her clothing blown off her, and long, black hair flicked across his mouth, as she half turned to look back at the carnage slowly emerging from the fog.

"Hold on there, luv. Did it hit clean on The Dwellings?"

"Aye, into t' middle yard." She clawed at him. "For Jesus' sake, get me boys out."

Throughout the raid, Conor and Mont, with the Rescue Squad, sweated and cursed their way into the ruins, sickened frequently, occasionally triumphant when they brought out the living, until in the early morning, a filthy, bloodstained Conor went back to the post to write out his report. New orphans, new widows, new cripples and a band of homeless. And what for? What was it in truth all about? God's curse on them all. He rubbed his torn and dirty hands on his overalls and reached for his pencil.

viii

Arms round each other, Gwen and Mari cowered on the cellar steps, certain that each strident screech above their heads would be the last thing they would ever hear.

The petrifying crash which destroyed The Dwellings made both of them scream. Tinkling glass and a rushing draught told them that the windows had blown in.

"Me sitting room! Me aspidistra!" Gwen wailed. Her Holy of Holies would be exposed to the weather – and thieves!

Mari began to cry.

The roar of the attack on the city centre was undiminished, but locally it was as if everything held its breath, as if the explosion of the land-mine had taken everything with it. Gwen and Mari loosed their grip on each other and raised their heads.

The quiet was broken by a frantic banging on the back door. "Missus, missus! Come quick," a boy's voice cried.

Patrick! Mari scrambled to her feet.

98

Her mother caught her by her bare ankle. "You stay here, miss. I'll go."

In the pink light coming from between the flapping remains of the blackout curtains, it was easy to see the familiar terrain of the brick-tiled kitchen. She flung open the back door. Five shadows tumbled in together, wailing like forgotten babies.

Gwen surveyed five shocked faces, in the uncertain light. "For Heaven's sake, what's to do?"

"It's Mam. She's hurt real bad," Patrick gulped. "Coom and help her."

Gwen swallowed. "Where is she?"

"She's lyin' by t' front step. Ah can't move her. Coom quick." The usually bumptious Patrick was beside himself, his face ashen.

Crowded close to him, the other children broke into loud howls. Ruby led the hullabaloo. Her mother, her only defence against the terror of the raids, was lying inert at the door of her home; and Ruby was convinced that all the houses would collapse any minute and she would again be buried.

Despite Gwen's own nervousness and confusion, the sickly smell of the children's unwashed bodies penetrated to her. Repulsed by it, she snapped at them, "Now you be quiet. I'll get a candle and go and have a look at your mam."

As the candle was lit, the howls tailed off into small sobs. The flame showed the small, barefoot crew in more detail. They all had white rivulets down their dirty faces.

For safety's sake, Gwen decided that the children could not return to their home with her; the gunfire was too heavy. She lit another candle and handed it to

Patrick. "Sit on the cellar steps with Mari – all of you. Get a move on, now. It's not safe up here. And mind your feet on the floor – there's glass all over. I'll be back in a minute."

Ruby, dragging a protesting Michael, led the way timidly. Patrick wiped the tears from his face, put on a defiant air and stood on the top step, leaning one shoulder against the wall to stop himself shaking.

Mari half smiled at him as she looked up the steps, but he did not even glance at her. She felt unexpectedly hurt. She turned her attention to Ruby. Gosh, how she smelled.

The clangour of fire-engine bells came clearly through the roar of the blitz, as Gwen, candle in hand, hesitated in her front doorway. What would she find next door?

A string of incendiaries slithered down a short distance away. Vicious pencils of flak suddenly peppered the road in front of her. She bobbed back into the hall. The candle blew out. With it still in her hand, she crept down the two carefully whitened steps of her own front entrance, as if by making no sound she could outwit the German pilots. Then she turned into the immediately adjacent front doorway of the Donnellys and stared into their hall. In dismay, she dropped the dead candle and it rattled away on the pavement.

Just inside, Ellen half lay, half sat, against the weathered door. One hand was flung across her breast. Her eyes, wide with shock, stared at the wall opposite her.

"Oh, my goodness!" Gwen took the two steps in one stride and knelt down by the woman. "Mrs Donnelly? Are you hurt?"

There was no reply. Gwen put out a careful hand and

touched her face. She did not move. The body was surrounded by the effluvium of human excrement, and a primeval fear of death clutched at Gwen's throat. In an agony of indecision, she glanced up at the small piece of sky she could see above the roofs opposite; in the flushed torment there, the battle raged on. Her breath came in short pants and she wanted to run away, out of Liverpool, away from the dirty horde on her cellar steps, away from this scarifying hulk of a woman. But there was nowhere to run to; even the street across the doorstep was a death-trap.

She took a big breath and pulled herself together. How did one make absolutely certain that a person was dead? She might still be alive – in shock – wounded only.

A resonant bang nearby, followed immediately by a shower of bricks and mortar on the doorstep, galvanised Gwen into action. Still kneeling, she leaned forward and tried to heave Ellen further into the hall. Ellen's arms flopped and her whole body reeled towards Gwen's tiny frame. In horror, Gwen let go and scrambled to her feet. Ellen slumped to the floor.

Doing her best not to vomit, and risking the descent of further missiles, she ran a few steps to the nearest street shelter and called hopefully through the doorway, "Anybody there?" But only a faint echo came from its stinking darkness.

She ran back to her own house and scuttled through the length of it. On the cellar steps, the children were sitting as rigidly as images; one little boy was crying heartily. At the sound of her footfall they turned to look up at her, the whites of their eyes gleaming in the candlelight.

"I'm going through the alleyway to Mr Baker's next door but one," she told them quickly. "To get some help for your mum. You all stay close, now. Everything's going to be all right."

She ran through the brick-walled back yard, out of the tall, plank gate and down the alley, which, with its narrowness and high walls, seemed to offer more protection than the front street. She reckoned the Baker family, also, would be in the basement and they would hear her knock more easily if she tried the back door.

"Mr Baker," she shrieked, above the rat-tat-tat of machine-guns. Fearfully she glanced upwards and then renewed her bangs with her fists.

"Wasser marrer?" inquired a richly Liverpool voice, as the door was opened a narrow crack.

"It's Mrs Thomas. Mrs Donnelly's hurt bad and I can't lift her into the house meself. And Mr Donnelly's on duty and me husband's in Bootle." The words poured out, as she wrung her hands helplessly.

The door swung open immediately to reveal, in the light of a kerosene lamp, an elderly man who looked, thought Gwen, a bit like a tortoise wrapped in a dressing-gown.

The wide mouth in the crumpled face opened. "Step in, step in. Let me get me slippers and tell Mother." He padded away, towards the cellar door.

Gwen thankfully entered the kitchen and shut the door behind her. By some fluke of the blast, Mr Baker's kitchen window was still intact. As fear gave way to resentment, she wondered crossly why her windows should always be those to be broken. Why should she get landed with someone wounded? And have to let in five disgusting kids?

Mr Baker came panting up the cellar steps again, his dressing-gown now tightly belted, his misshapen feet encased in carpet slippers.

"Where is she?" he inquired.

"By her front door. It's open."

"Coom through then."

Seething with suppressed vexation at the unfairness of fate, she followed him through his front door, round the tiny bay windows of his home and that of the Donnellys, and up the latter's front steps. From behind the closed door of the kitchen, Sarge began to bark.

Mr Baker put the lamp down on the floor. Very gently he lifted Ellen's arm. A piece of shrapnel was deeply embedded in her side. He held her wrist for a moment, but there was no sign of a pulse.

He got laboriously to his feet. "Let's get her in and shut the door."

As a postman, he was used to lifting awkward weights and he soon pulled her along the bare wooden floor, by putting his hands under her arms from the back. Then he quietly shut the front door; it cut off a lot of the noise from outside.

He looked carefully at the wound. It had bled little and he toyed with the idea of pulling out the piece of shrapnel. Better to leave her as she was, he decided. With womanly care, he turned her on one side to look at her back. Another sliver protruded for about an inch from under one shoulder-blade.

"I reckon she were hit first in her chest and she half turned into the house, and the second piece hit her in the back," he said to a shocked Gwen. "She's dead for sure." He laid the body flat on its back and gently closed the staring eyes. Then he glanced round him,

103

puzzled. "Where's all the kids?"

Gwen licked her white lips. "All in my house, with our Mari."

"That's proper kind of you, Mrs Thomas." He took a crumpled handkerchief out of his dressing-gown pocket and, with a grimace of distaste, wiped Ellen's life-blood from his hands. Gwen stood uncertainly before him, her hands clasped tightly together. Her irritation had faded and she felt numb, unable to make herself think.

"It's more'n anybody's life's worth to go up to the post in this," Baker went on heavily. "As soon as the All-Clear sounds, I'll get up there and tell him – and get some help to move her." He rubbed his almost non-existent chin, grey with a day's beard, and then smelled the dried blood still on his hands. Sickened, he dropped them to his sides. "The kids'll do fine with you." He looked down kindly at the small wraith in front of him. "Five of them, isn't there? Poor little buggers – excuse the language."

At the remembrance of the repellent collection sitting on her well-scrubbed steps, Gwen felt nauseated again. But she could not, in all conscience, send them back home, while their dead mother lay where she did. "Donnelly'll have to get a relation to come in and look after them," she said.

"Aye," he agreed. "I'll leave it to you how you tell them."

Gwen stared up at him, aghast. How could *she* tell them? Surely it was not her responsibility? But Mr Baker's mind had gone on to other things, and he said, "I'll let the dog out in the morning, if Donnelly isn't back."

In her own house, she faced the children, as they rose

expectantly from their uncomfortable seats on the steps. Ruby held a sleeping Michael; she looked as if she might faint.

Mari was in the kitchen, calmly making cups of cocoa for their guests, while the early morning breeze fluttered her long white nightgown and made the gas jet dance.

The sounds from outside indicated that the attack had shifted slightly to another part of the town, though the rhythmic beat of engines overhead continued.

Gwen looked resentfully at the little crew and cleared her throat uneasily, while the children waited like marble statues in a cemetery. She said carefully, "Your ma's hurt rather bad. Mr Baker next door but one is looking after her. He'll send her to the hospital." She cleared her throat again, some pity for them seeping into her. "You're not to worry. Everything's goin' to be all right."

Relief dawned on Ruby's face. She said to Nora and Brendy, aged 7 and 6 respectively, "See, I told yer so. We're all goin' to have a nice cup o' cocoa, and when the raid's over, we'll go home to bed." She turned to Gwen. "I could go to Mam now – the kids'll be all right with you and Mari."

"No. No," Gwen responded hastily. "Your mam wants you to stay to comfort them."

When she turned to fuss round the cocoa maker, Patrick followed her and stood squarely in front of her. His face was grim and the fine, blue eyes looked at her fearlessly. "I *know*," he said scornfully.

"Well, don't you say nothin' for the minute," Gwen murmured out of the side of her mouth, like a convict. Then, feeling ashamed, she added, "I'm real sorry, lad." She felt like adding, I'm sorry for me, too.

Mari glanced up from her stirring, surprise and fear

mingled in her expression. Patrick's face crumbled, tears welled up again.

He's only about 13, Gwen thought, for all he's so big. Instinctively she moved towards him and put her hand on his shoulder. She tried to reassure him. "It'll be all right when your dad comes," she said.

Mari bit her lips to restrain her own desire to cry. She put four cups on a brightly printed tray, filled them and took them to the children on the steps. She said with forced cheerfulness, "Here you are, ducks."

When she turned back to pour out cocoa for her mother and Patrick, she saw with a pang of jealousy that her cold, fastidious parent was holding Patrick's head against her skimpy chest and crooning, "Never mind, luv, never mind." And Patrick, tough cruel Patrick, was actually crying as if his heart would break. Her own lips quivered, as she took down some more cups from their hooks.

Gwen herself was in torment. The children must stay with her until their mother's body was removed. That meant they would probably have to sleep the rest of the night in her house; and they probably had nits in their hair – she would have to burn the pillows afterwards, which would make David thoroughly angry because of the cost of new ones. But what else could she do?

She was personally revolted by their dirtiness; even this beautiful boy smelled as if he had never had a bath since he was born. With a sigh, she urged, "Have a cup o' cocoa, luv. Make you feel better." She took a cup from Mari and handed it to him. "What was your mam doin' at the door on a night like this?"

He took a small gulp of the scalding liquid. "There were a terrible bang – and then it were dead quiet, like.

106

So she run up to see if it were the houses opposite what were hit — 'cos they'd need our help, if they were." He faltered, and then went on, "I heard her cry out and I run up meself — and there she was on the floor — and she never said nothin' — and I knew." His cup rattled against his teeth, as he took another sip.

"God rest her." Gwen put her empty cup down on the drainboard. "We'd better get down the steps. You, too, Mari. We'll wash up tomorrow."

SUNDAY, 4 MAY 1941

Ruby's arms were stiff from holding the dead weight of young Michael. Every so often in his sleep, he would nuzzle into her non-existent breasts, looking for the comfort of his mother's milk. Then, frustrated, he would whimper and sleep again.

Patrick sat with eyes closed and fists clenched. He was tortured by the idea of his mother lying alone in the house next door. He wanted to go to her, look at her, try to wake her from her long sleep. But he was afraid of the demons in the sky, afraid of facing alone the fact of her death. After a while, his head fell forward, his mouth opened and he, too, slept.

Just before five o'clock, they all awoke with a jerk to a profound silence, except for Gwen who continued to snore.

Mari shook her mother's arm. "Ma, it's stopped. They've gone."

"Who? What?" Gwen jerked her head from against the cellar wall and blinked. She had been having a nightmare, a nightmare in which the whole house crawled away as a result of the infestation brought in by the Donnelly children. Through her fogged brain, she heard the long, thin cry of the All Clear.

"Phew!" she exclaimed. Then she gazed blearily down at the appalling weight of responsibility sitting on the inhospitable stone steps below her.

Brendy, aged 5, struggled awake and stood up on wobbling legs. He stared round the alien staircase and then roared tearfully, "Where's me mam?" He started to struggle past the knees of the other children, to get to the top of the steps, howling like a miserable dog. Nora, a year older, turned to follow him. She began to whimper. As she threatened to teeter backwards down the steps, Ruby grabbed her wrist.

"Leave me go," the child yelled savagely. She began to beat her big sister in the face with a small clenched fist.

Patrick got up slowly. With frightened, bloodshot eyes, he glanced down at his hostess and then at the other children. A curling spiral of unvented rage ran through him. "Brendy! You shut up or I'll clobber yez. Mam's been hurt and can't come to yez."

Brendy's howls came down a full octave, and Nora stopped trying to get a hold on Ruby's hair to tear it out; when Patrick decided to hit someone, he often distributed the favour throughout the family. Nora's white-lashed eyes narrowed and she made an obscene gesture at Ruby.

Patrick addressed his snivelling siblings again, his voice suddenly placating. "Mrs Thomas is going to let us stay here, aren't you, Mrs Thomas?" His eyes were on Gwen now, pleading, defeated.

Gwen was dizzy with lack of sleep and could not bring her mind into focus. She rubbed her face and then ran her fingers through her frizzy hair. She nodded. Even if Ellen Donnelly's body had been removed, the children would feel the absence of their mother more keenly in their own home and would ask more questions – and she did not want to have to break the news to them that they would never see her again. Better by far to keep them in her own home and let Donnelly do the job in the morning.

She stood up. Her whole body ached. And where was David in all this? He should be at home taking charge of everything. It was unfair that she should carry the whole burden. She began to simmer with resentment. And Emmie hadn't turned up either, to give her a hand.

"I want to pee," wailed Brendy, clutching at himself.

"For heaven's sake, take him down the yard," she ordered Patrick, as she yawned mightily. "Tut, he hasn't got any shoes on – lift him over the glass in the kitchen – and no socks neither – 'is poor little feet is purple."

It was as if Brendy's sad straits forced her awake. She turned to her drooping, equally sleepy daughter. "Mari, get the dustpan and brush, and get the glass off the kitchen floor, so the little boy – and the little girl – you ain't got no shoes neither, luv? – don't cut their feet."

Nora was not to be wooed by a kindly tone. She stuck her finger in her mouth and looked sulky. Gwen turned to Ruby. "And you, what's your name?"

"Ruby, missus." From beneath her shaggy fringe two sad eyes gleamed dully.

"Well, you got shoes on. You bring the baby upstairs with me, and we'll put him on a potty and then into bed. The little girl can wait in the living room a minute, till Patrick comes back with the little lad." She lifted a stiff, unyielding Nora up the stairs and deposited her on the living room hearthrug, which seemed to be clear of broken glass. The child ignored her and stared around the strange room.

Thankful that someone seemed to know what to do, Ruby trailed upstairs, a fretful, complaining Michael in her arms. She looked with awe at Emmie's bedroom into which she was ushered. Though its pretty, rose-covered curtains, which normally masked the blackout curtains, had been torn by glass, to Ruby it looked like a film star's bedroom. A matching curtain hung from a corner shelf, to make a wardrobe, and Ruby eyed its cascade of printed flowers wonderingly. The window glass had fallen in a rough heap beneath the sill, and Gwen leaned over it to slip the ripped blackout curtains across the casement.

Ruby shivered in the draught. She felt as if she had expended every scrap of energy she had, and she was sick with apprehension about her mother; she was silently counting the minutes until morning, when she could ask her father how she was and whether she could go to the hospital to see her.

Gwen pulled out a rose-wreathed chamber pot from under the bed. Michael objected violently to being held over it, and kicked and screamed. Gwen persisted until he made water – she was not going to have her beds soaked. A puddle was left on the heavily patterned linoleum. With the enraged child under one arm, she pulled back the bedclothes, to expose the whitest sheets Ruby had ever seen, and then shoved the little boy into bed.

"Now you be quiet," she ordered sharply. "Your Ruby's going to come and lie by you and make you warm, aren't you Ruby?" Ruby assented and started to climb into bed, shoes, dress and all, but Gwen looked at her in such a scandalised fashion, that she hastily reversed herself and pulled off her faded cotton dress and hooked it on to the bed knob. Then she kicked her worn lace-up shoes under the bed.

"That's better," Gwen approved.

Emboldened by the approbation, Ruby inquired, "Me mam? Which hospital did they take her to?"

Gwen looked at the whey-faced, skinny child nearly as tall as herself, the bony chest half-covered by a grubby vest. She knew nothing of the silent terror with which Ruby had faced the night; she saw only that the girl was swaying on her feet. She replied carefully, "Mr Baker was going to see about her being taken to hospital. I don't know which one, though. But you don't have to worry. Mr Baker is proper kind, and Mrs Baker will have gone in to comfort her, until the ambulance arrived." The latter statement made her realise what an accomplished liar she could be, but she cringed at telling the brutal truth. "Now you get into bed, and in no time your Dad'll be here and tell you all about it. Mr Baker was going to send a message up to the post as soon as the All Clear went."

Ruby smiled weakly and climbed into the wonderful bed. Two pillows and real white sheets – and blankets. Gwen tucked her and the complaining child into the bed and left them, taking the candle with her. As soon as she had left the room, Ruby got out again and felt around for the chamber pot.

"Our Emmie is going to have to make do on the sitting room sofa, when she comes in," Gwen told Patrick, who was waiting by the cold fireplace in the living room. He was still holding Brendy. Brendy's head had sunk on to his brother's shoulder and he was sound asleep. Patrick had managed to light the gaslight which hung from the middle of the ceiling, and a bright shaft lit up the back yard. Gwen tushed, and ran to the window to close the dusty blackout curtains over the flushed dawn sky. The breeze blew them up into the room, so she hastily picked up her work-basket and balanced it on the sill, to hold them down. A clatter of glass dropped into the kitchen rubbish-bin told her that Mari had done what she had been ordered to do. Gwen sighed, and turned to survey her remaining unwanted guests. "Now, what to do with you?"

"Dunno," responded Patrick mechanically. Round and round inside his head, went the picture of his mother as he had last seen her; nothing else touched him.

"I know. I'll put the girl here ..." She paused, and then asked, "What's your name?"

A malevolent, pinched face was turned up towards her. "I'm Nora," the tight lips spat out.

Gwen recoiled slightly. What a horrid, wizened-faced brat. "I'll put you and the little lad here — Brendy, isn't it? — in our Mari's bed. Mari can sleep with me." Not for all the wealth in China could she bring herself to put any of the children in her own huge double bed; she would never sleep comfortable in it again, she told herself. "And you, Patrick, can kip down on the sofa here. I'll get a blanket out for you. But first bring the kids upstairs."

She preceded him, the candle flame streaming a thin line of smoke behind her. "The whole place smells of smoke," she remarked over her shoulder, "but it's all from outside. Nothin' to worry about."

Patrick did not care what the place smelled of, as long as he could lie down, curl up and try to obliterate the fact that his maddening, bossy, beloved mam was dead.

Nora's stony expression relaxed and she followed Gwen up the carpeted staircase, sidling along like a stray dog in search of something to eat, sniffing, touching everything. She went straight to the dressing

116

table and, standing on tiptoe, reached over to pick up Mari's most prized possession, a china lady in a crinoline.

"You put that down!" Gwen's face was dark with immediate anger. "You don't touch nothin' in this house, young lady."

Nora glanced up at her with pale, expressionless eyes. Slowly she opened her hand and let the china figure drop. It broke into three pieces.

"You naughty little vixen," Gwen shrieked at her. She caught the child by the shoulder and gave her a sound slap on her bottom. "Our Mari'll be broken-hearted, she will, you little devil. Get your frock off and get into bed afore I mairder you."

With a look of complete satisfaction on her face, Nora removed her dress, to show only a pair of tattered knickers.

Gwen pulled a chamber pot from under the bed, this one with a pattern of violets to match the mauve curtains. "You pull them panties down and pay a call," she ordered a bridling Nora. Nora did not seem to hear, so Gwen took her by the shoulder and shoved her down on to it.

Patrick had stood with Brendy in his arms, waiting for Gwen to finish with Nora. He was used to loud voices and slaps and to Nora being a trial to his mother; it was nothing out of the ordinary.

Boiling with rage, Gwen whipped back the bedclothes and he thankfully put Brendy, fully-clothed, into the bed. "And you get in, miss, and let's have no more trouble," she ordered Nora. Nora, knowing the precise breaking point of most adults, felt it was wise to comply.

Outside the bedroom, Gwen and Patrick came face to

face with a bewildered, sulky Mari; she did not like her room being taken over by two dirty kids. "You get into our bed, Mari – on your father's side. I don't know what we do when he comes home. And I don't know what he's going to say."

She opened a drawer of a fine oak chest on the landing, one of the pieces of furniture appropriated from Emmie's home, and took out two thin, but clean, blankets. "You go make yourself comfy on the sofa in the living room," she told Patrick.

She had to repeat her command before Patrick took any notice. As Mari passed, she had caught his hand and squeezed it. "I'm sorry," she had whispered, and he realised with a gleam of comfort that she understood how he felt. He wanted to cry on her shoulder. To Gwen he said, "Yes, missus."

While Gwen lay, rigid and awake, beside Mari, Mari suddenly remarked, "You know, mam, it's over half an hour since the All-Clear went, and Auntie Emmie isn't in yet."

"Your aunt's big enough to take care of herself. She'll be in just now – probably gossiping somewhere." Gwen could not take any more; she had been tried beyond endurance, and the very thought of Emmie and her Robert added to her grumpiness. The sly bitch and her greediness about the furniture.

Though Emmie went through the motions of being a good sister-in-law, her bitter resentment against Gwen's refusal to help with her sick parents was all too apparent. Mari's reminder that Emmie had not yet returned made Gwen feel that she did not care if the woman never came back; yet, underneath it all, her Methodist conscience smote her hard – Emmie had carried a terrible load which Gwen could have eased. Angrily, she turned over in her bed. If Emmie were dead, she would be free of the remainder of her own sins of omission. Savagely, she *wished* her dead, as she lay seething with frustration at her current predicaments.

Suddenly, as a new horror occurred to her, she sat up in bed beside the sleeping Mari. She had never looked to see what had happened to her precious sitting-room – the aspidistra in its big, green pottery bowl, set on a table in the bay window, the settee and two easy chairs which she had recently recovered herself in bright orange-flowered cretonne, and the piano, still not quite paid for, which Mari was learning to play, taught at a shilling a lesson by Mrs Cooper down the road. Was it all ruined by the blast?

She could not bear it, if it were all spoiled. She started to turn back the bedclothes, to go down and look, and then flung them back over herself. She could not endure to know now, and she turned her face into her pillow and quietly wept herself to sleep.

Patrick, too, cried – into the patchwork cushion on the sagging horsehair sofa. The pain was so great that it was as if the shrapnel in his mother's body had pierced him.

A light tread descending the staircase made him lift his head abruptly. Was Mari coming down?

"Pat, where are you?"

"Here, Rube." He let his head fall back on to the cushion.

"I were so scared, Pat." She crept towards him through the darkened room and knelt down by the sofa. He sat up and her seeking arms went round him.

"It were the worst raid." Patrick's voice was more gentle.

"I'm worried about our mam. Mrs Thomas don't say much."

Patrick ran his tongue round his lips. Then he said very softly, "She's dead, Rube. Didn't you realise it?"

"Oh," she gasped, putting her hand against her mouth to control an involuntary shriek. "No, Pat. I thought she'd fainted."

She put her head down on his blanketed lap and he could feel her shivering. Then she began to sob. He sat stiffly under her weight. "Don't, Rube," he muttered. "Don't."

"I can't help it. What are we goin' to do without Mam?"

"Dunno," he replied thickly. But he did know. It happened all the time when mothers died. Ruby would take her mother's place. Like many another motherless girl, she would learn to wash and cook for the family and tend little Michael. He was glad he wasn't a girl. He lived for the day when he would be big enough, hefty enough, to go down to the docks and stand in the pen, to be picked again and again for work, because he was the biggest and best. And he would bring home real wages and take a pretty girl, like Mari, to the pictures. Ruby would slave most of her life for nothing, because her mother was dead.

No wonder Ruby wept.

ii

During this terrifying Saturday night and Sunday

morning, while Gwen coped with her unwelcome visitors, five hundred German bombers converged on the already stricken city, with orders to wipe it out, make it unusable by the convoys of ships from the United States.

They were met by Defiant fighter planes darting bravely in and out of the searchlight beams, in an effort to confuse and harass them. But the Defiants were too slow and their guns were wrongly placed, and not all the gallantry and skill of their crews could compensate for the planes' deficiencies.

There were not many seamen in the canteen that night, nor had the firewatchers come in for their accustomed snacks. Deckie Dick was seated in his usual place at the centre table, from which vantage point he could look out of the window to watch the passing scene and also observe all that was going on in the canteen itself. He idly shuffled the deck of cards, from which he derived his nickname, from one hand to the other, as he regaled a bored younger merchant seaman with the story of the rescue work he had participated in the night before.

When the first bombs whistled down, neither staff nor customers sought the shelter of the basement, but when suddenly the attack seemed particularly near and intense, everybody dropped what they were doing and fled for the stairs. As they tumbled down the curving flight, the window shutters flew open with an angry rattle; the front door was blown off its hinges and shot across the canteen, followed by a torrent of sand from burst sandbags. As the blast receded, the door flew out again, to crash against the lamp post on the pavement.

Miss Piggot, one of the volunteers, had tripped on the

121

bottom step and fallen, taking a swearing, flailing Scot down with her. Now, they both picked themselves up off the stone floor and ruefully rubbed their knees. "My poor stockings," wailed Miss Piggot, lifting her skirts to look at the tears. Mrs Robinson pushed her to one side and quickly closed the stout door which guarded the foot of the staircase. She sat down on one of the benches and smiled at a thin, pimpled Royal Naval rating already perched there. He was rolling himself a cigarette, with trembling fingers. "Soon be over," she told him comfortingly. He replied wryly, "I'd rather be at sea." And her plump face creased with laughter.

"Phew!" exclaimed Emmie, as she sat down by Deckie Dick. "That were close." She shivered and rubbed her bare forearms, as if she were cold.

"Aye. Looks as if we're in for a bad night." He looked tired beneath the grey stubble of two days' beard. As a night watchman, he was not used to heavy physical labour and he had spent the previous night heaving beams and chunks of stone out of the way of rescue squads. As he glanced down at Emmie's anxious face, he was thinking he would be thankful to be back at work on Monday night, when he could, between his rounds, kip down in a warm corner of the warehouse which he watched. He leaned his bald head, with its fringe of white hair, against the whitewashed wall and closed his eyes against the glare of the single electric light bulb hanging from the ceiling. Pity the lodging house in which he lived was so noisy; otherwise he could have slept in a bit longer that morning.

As the raid progressed, the electric light began to flicker, so Mrs Robinson opened her capacious handbag and took out a candle and some matches. She lit it and then glued it down on to the corner table, by drips of its own wax. Then she blew it out.

The uproar outside became intense. "Good thing they're bringing in mining engineers, to help out," remarked Dick, his eyes still closed. "They can advise the heavy-rescue men."

Emmie nodded and leaned forward to rest her face on her hands, to stop herself shaking.

Mrs Robinson turned to the taciturn countess, who was seated stiffly opposite her, her ankles crossed neatly, her skirts precisely arranged around her. "I wish I had shut the canteen at ten o'clock," she remarked. "I had an uneasy feeling this morning that there would be another raid tonight."

The countess looked down her Norman nose and sniffed delicately. "On no account should you have closed. It would show that we are intimidated." Her wonderful diamond rings flashed, as she dismssed the Luftwaffe with an impatient gesture.

The naval rating drew on his cigarette and stared at her. Proper rum old dame, she was. If he were as rich as she looked, he would be thirty miles away from any place like Liverpool.

A gaunt and hunched ship's stoker, sitting cross-legged on the floor playing cards with three others, suddenly looked up. "Can yer smell smoke?" he inquired nervously of the company.

"Be funny if we couldn't, after last night's effort," grunted one of his fellow players. He shuffled his cards secretly, close to his face.

"I mean in here," the stoker responded irritably. Holding his cards to his chest, he got up, went to the door and opened it. Conversation ceased. He crept up a couple of steps and peered around, then bolted down again, as a huge swish followed by a roar and the sound of tumbling masonry indicated a hit nearby.

"Shut the door, you bloody fool," shouted a highly alarmed voice.

"Had to take a look-see," grumbled the equally shaken stoker. "T' canteen might've bin bairnin' over our heads."

Emmie fidgeted unhappily beside Deckie Dick. Why planners never put lavatories in air raid shelters was beyond her. It was certain that they must live far away from air raids; otherwise they would have known that the banshee wail of the warning was like a switch turning on your waterworks. She wondered if some of the fellows felt as she did, and she giggled shakily.

Deckie Dick opened his eyes. "What's ticklin' yer, luv?"

She blushed and whispered into his ear. He laughed, and replied, "I'm in the same boat."

The card players had been murmuring together. Now the owner of the pack knocked them together and put them in his back pocket. They got up and stretched. "Got to get back to the ship," they informed Mrs Robinson, "raid or no raid."

Mrs Robinson, alarmed, half rose from her bench. "You can't go out in this, Mr Petersen. No one would expect you to." But she read the panic in their eyes, and she sank down again. A ship out in the river might seem a safer place than the bedlam surrounding them.

Their opening of the door let in a dull roar, punctuated by occasional shouts and the sound of lorries from the docks being driven in low gear, as drivers tried to get themselves and their loads to safety.

They scurried up the steps, only to throw themselves flat on the littered floor at the top, as another deafening detonation made the old building shudder and sent bits of plaster flying from the ceiling. The subsequent rumble of falling masonry confirmed their opinion that, if they *could* get away, they preferred to be aboard ship. Who wanted to be buried under eight floors of eighteenth-century stone blocks?

As they scrambled over the remains of the sandbag wall, they were shaken to see that the street was as light as day.

"Get under cover," shouted an irate auxiliary policeman, running towards them half sideways, like a crab, to gain the greatest protection from the office walls.

The men took no notice of him and sped past him, bent on reaching the overhead railway which might well still be running and would take them south, away from what appeared to be the raid's main targets. In so doing, they saved their lives. With her face buried in her lap and her arms clasped over her head for maximum protection, Emmie prayed that Robert was safely out of the port. She jabbed Deckie Dick with her elbow, and shouted above the noise, "Do you think Robbie will've sailed yet?"

Dick paused before answering. He knew that the *Malakand* had not yet left dock and he knew what she was being loaded with. But why add to the girl's worries? He answered her quite cheerfully, "She may have got away this mornin'."

Relieved, Emmir returned to worrying about the need to go to the lavatory.

In No. 2 Huskisson, Robbie heaved the last of a series

of spitting incendiaries off the foredeck and into the water.

"Watch it!" shrieked one of his mates, and pointed upwards.

Robbie whipped round.

A barrage balloon, half deflated, loosed from its moorings, was settling into the rigging.

Someone shrieked to Robbie, "Get away. It'll explode."

Robbie scrambled aft and with the rest of the crew watched helplessly as the grey monster was pulled and pushed by the breeze. A particularly strong gust loosened it and it flopped on to the for'ard deck.

Several men started towards it, but they were grabbed and held back by more cautious seamen.

A second later, the grey, silky mass burst into flames, a huge, scarifying ball of fire.

Regardless of the deadly cargo beneath their feet, the officers ordered hoses out and for fifteen agonised minutes the crew deluged the roaring fire with water, while more incendiaries were scattered down on to the hapless freighter.

A Nazi bomber swooped along the nearby dock sheds dropping a further load of incendiaries. Orange flowers of flame burst from the roofs, and in minutes a mighty conflagration stretched from Huskisson to Seaforth, like a brilliant multicoloured curtain. The wind generated by the fire sent huge fingers of flame out to the boat, and the crew found themselves surrounded by fire licking along the ship from stem to stern. Robbie could see the raw terror which struck him, reflected in the eyes of the others; yet they and the auxiliary firemen sent to help them held on to their hoses until, through the noise of the blaze, came the firm voice of the shore relief master, "Abandon ship."

Black, singed and panting, they regrouped on the dockside and were immediately put to work jetting water into the holds, while a special tender was sent for, to bring oxy-acetylene apparatus to the boat.

"Goin' to try scuttlin' her – cut a hole in her side," a fireman said to Robbie, as they sought to hold a wriggling hose towards the ship.

"Aye, they'd better be quick," Robbie gasped, "or we're all for Kingdom Come, and half of Liverpool as well."

iii

There was a fumbling at the door of the canteen shelter. Mrs Robinson hastened to open it, and an air raid warden entered in a puff of smoke. His tin hat was askew and he was swaying with fatigue. "Just checkin' who's here," he assured them, and, pointing to each person, he counted the number present.

"What's happening up there?" asked Mrs Robinson. Her face was wan and her lipstick smudged, giving her a clownlike appearance.

The warden flopped down on the end of a bench and the weary shelterers turned towards him. He took off his tin hat to rub his bald head. Emmie noticed that his trousers were thick with dust and there were holes in the knees.

"Lewis's store is a raging inferno," he said to Mrs Robinson, in answer to her query. "Must've lost most of their firewatchers. T' firemen is stuck for water." His dispirited voice lifted a little, and he grinned, "T' fire brigade has pumped all the water out of the Adelphi's swimming bath into Lewis's. That'll larn that snobs' paradise."

A ripple of laughter at the expense of the city's finest hotel went through the company.

Too bad about the firewatchers, thought Emmie, but if you didn't laugh at what was funny you'd soon go mad.

"Our telephone at the post is out," he went on more soberly. "Bloody havoc without it. Seen a couple of post office engineers just now, slinging lines every which way, to get us connected up again. And there's another two of them sittin' in a crater right in the street here, splicin' telephone lines as calm as if they was havin' afternoon tea at Lyons'." He stood up and stretched. "It's a bloody miracle they're not dead."

"Should we try to move out of here?" asked Mrs Robinson.

"Nay. You're safer here than anywhere. South Castle Street, at the back here, is a shambles, what with fire and direct hits. I'll come back and tell you, if the firemen think you should move."

"Do they need men up there?" inquired a lanky individual in battered beige denim trousers, as he got up clumsily from the floor.

"Not now, they don't. They will when the All Clear goes, though."

"Not tonight, Josephine. Sit down again," cracked a wit.

The warden clapped his helmet back on to his head, grinned in a friendly way and clumped back up the steps.

A collective sigh went through the company and they settled back to wait again.

The light went out. Mrs Robinson quietly lit the candle. Its flame seemed to emphasize the lined faces of the men and women, picking out a drooping eyelid, a blackened tooth, the sole of a shoe with a hole in it, the glitter of a cheap ring on a chapped hand.

From the gloom, a forlorn young voice informed its neighbour, "Me leave's up at eight o'clock tomorrer mornin'. Got to be back in camp by then. I were on me way to the station when this lot started. Ah coom in 'ere, thinkin' it'd all blow over in an hour."

"You got a bleedin' hope, mate. You live around here?" Deckie Dick inquired.

"Aye, wi' me gran. Lives in Pitt Street. She were scared enough last night, without this on top."

Emmie remembered that a heavily built youth in battledress had scuttled into the canteen when the first bomb fell. Poor lad. No more'n eighteen, he must be.

The young voice continued, a little muffled from the owner's face being buried in his lap, his tin hat perched atop the back of his head. "Dunno whether to go back home or go t' station and show up late at camp anyways."

"Report back to camp," rumbled several voices, and Deckie Dick added, "Aye, you'll be in real trouble if you don't – absent without leave, they'll jump you for. There's people as'll look after your gran." He raised his head from his lap, to look at the crouching boy. "I'll go meself, if you like. You give me your address and her address. I'll go and see her tomorrer – and I'll write to you straight away. You'll get it the next day."

The boy glanced up quickly at Dick's ruddy,

good-natured visage, faintly lit by the candle. "She'd be proper pleased. She's real lonely," he said somewhat more cheerfully.

With Mrs Robinson's fountain pen, he clumsily printed the addresses on the back of a café receipt and passed the paper to Dick.

Dick folded it up carefully, put it into a shabby wallet and returned the wallet to his back pocket. Above the wallet he pushed in a grubby comb; he always said that a comb was the best defence against pickpockets or even plain losing your wallet. Now he thought that it would not hurt him to go and sit with some old Irish biddy for an hour, to help a youngster. It would be something to do. He had been lonely ever since his wife's death a year earlier.

The noise outside gradually lessened, as if the main target of the raid had been shifted. Ears pricked and heads were cautiously raised.

Emmie thought for a second that she heard women's voices outside. Women's Voluntary Service van, she guessed, feeding the firemen and the wardens. My, she could use a cup of tea herself.

"I'm goin' upstairs," announced Deckie Dick heavily. He winked down at Emmie.

Emmie promptly jumped up. "I'll come, too."

It was evident from a lewd gesture on the part of Deckie Dick where he was going, and Mrs Robinson said apprehensively, "Emmie, you should not go upstairs yet; it's too dangerous."

Emmie was immediately defensive. Nobody was going to tell her any more what she should or should not do; she'd had a bowlful of that from her parents. Besides, if she didn't go soon, she'd wet her knickers.

130

Emmie smoothed her skirts and tossed her head. "I'll be all right, Mrs Robinson. Dickie'll look after me." She glanced teasingly at Dick, as if single-handedly he could force the Luftwaffe into retreat.

Left to himself, Dickie would have run up the stairs and urinated just outside the front door, and then returned as fast as his tired legs would have carried him. But Emmie would be counting on his going through to the backyard privies.

The man sitting next to Dick yawned and glanced at Emmie. "You lucky bastard," he muttered to Dick.

Dick laughed. He felt that at his age it was a compliment.

In the middle of the wrecked canteen, they paused to look through the gaping hole where the window had been, at the dancing shadows on the wall of the building opposite.

"Good Heavens!" Emmie exclaimed fearfully. "There must be an awful fire behind our building."

"T' warden said as we were OK. Come on now, quick." His words were nearly drowned in the rumble of a series of bomb explosions, as the Luftwaffe took a run at the centre of the fire they had started alongside No.2 Huskisson.

Except for glassless windows, all the buildings round the light well seemed undamaged, though the sky glowed red above them. They ran across the cobbled yard, glass crunching under their feet, and with sighs of relief paid the long-delayed calls.

Close to hand, the tumbling roar of a wall collapsing brought them both out at a run, Emmie still pulling up her knickers. It buried the warden beneath its shattered stone, as he ran along the street. Another bomb exploded in the fire at the back of them, sending a shower of sparks into the air. Emmie screamed.

A further swish and crash made Dick hurl her to the ground, his plump body on top of her.

"Jesus, save us!" she shrieked, as she hit the unfriendly cobblestones. She clung to him.

"Keep yer head down. God, that was …"

With a deafening crash, the whole of the canteen was blown out.

An agonised blow on the forehead made her yell again, as she and Dick were lifted by the blast. Then, clinging to Dick, she was rolling and falling. She saw the ground beneath them crack and open in a tremendous yawn, as if in some unearthly dream. Dick seemed to slip from her, as she hit sliding rubble and then half fell, half slid, down and down on to a shuddering floorspace, mercilessly bumped and bruised as she went. She was aware, in a split second, of the earth closing over her as if a great door had been slammed, of a dreadful weight on the lower part of her body and of an ear-rending storm of noise. Then silence, except, from nearby, thin horrifying screams like souls crying out in Dante's *Inferno*, as she sank into oblivion.

iv

In smothering dust, Emmie fought for breath. As she coughed and choked and spat, the pain in her head was all-encompassing. She endeavoured to raise a hand to clear her face of rubble, but both hands were pinned against her stomach by a huge, warm solid mass; she shuddered as she realised what it might be.

She tried shaking her head and then moaned when the movement not only added to the pain in her head, but pulled her hair as well; its longer strands appeared to be caught under some unyielding weight.

Suddenly she sneezed enormously, her nose ran and she could breathe a little more easily. Small anonymous pieces of rubble, dislodged by the sneeze, slipped down the sides of her face.

As greater consciousness seeped back into her and she laboured for air amid the cloying dust, the dawning knowledge that she was buried made her tremble violently.

She became aware of stinging pain all over her face, in addition to the throbbing in her head. Cautiously, fearfully, she opened her eyes a slit. She could see nothing.

She was blind! She was sure of it. The trickles she could feel from her eyes must be blood, not tears. She screamed in horror, a howl of pure terror. Dust again entered her throat and the screams became strangled coughs. Then the pain in her head overwhelmed her and she faded into unconsciousness again.

She came round slowly, aware now of being surrounded by reverberating, booming noise. The ground under her, if it were ground and not a floor of some kind, vibrated continuously, adding to her own shuddering. The sagging weight on her body also moved slightly. At first her fogged mind believed the movement was also caused by the noise; then a large breath was exhaled, followed by a series of coughs.

In sudden joy, she croaked, "Is that you, Dick?"

Though she got no reply because of the paroxysm of coughing, she felt a hand run down the side of her and heard a faint rattle of what sounded like pebbles falling as the same hand apparently explored a little further. Then, with a satisfied grunt as the coughs eased, the body carefully rolled over until it was positioned tightly beside her. A series of muffled curses in a man's voice came from close to her ear. Thankfully she took a larger breath, to ease her constricted lungs, only to set off a further desperate coughing which threatened to cause her to vomit, as powdered plaster cloyed her throat again.

Above her, there was a series of ominous creaks, and in the distance the sound of water trickling. The surrounding uproar seemed to have decreased.

"Hold it, luv. Hold it," came a frantic whisper. "Yer noise'll bring the whole issue down on us. Breath shallow, if you can."

She did her best to control the coughing, lifting a hand, tingling with pins and needles, to cover her mouth. Between efforts to clear her throat, she giggled hysterically, "Oh, Dickie, I'm so glad you're here."

"*I'm* not," came the dry response. The body packed tightly beside her fidgeted slightly. "God spare us!"

She began to laugh wildly at this, only to choke again and to have her hair pulled painfully as she moved.

"Hold your hush, luv," he cajoled softly and caught one of her hands as if to comfort her.

She sobered as best she could. "Are you hurt, Dick?" she inquired hoarsely.

"Not much, I don't think. Wind kicked out o' me." His breath came laboriously. "Feel like I did after a fight once, in a bar in New York. Got beat up." He squeezed her hand. "How about you?"

He could feel her trembling increase. Carefully, he lifted an arm round her, as she whimpered, "Dickie, I think I'm blinded. I can't see anything. Me hair is caught under something – and me face is all wet and sticky. I'm afraid to touch it."

He did not reply for a moment and then he assured her, "Well nobody could see in this dark. Are you sure? Open and close yer eyelids. Do they work? You're lying on your back, aren't you?"

"I can move me lids. They're awful sore."

"Humph. Well, try touching round them, very lightly, to see if the eyes is still in their sockets."

Sickened by the implication, she nevertheless moved her fingers cautiously round her cheeks and over her closed lids. She moved her eyes from right to left and then blinked. "They seem all right," she announced with marked relief. "They're running like mad."

"Aye, you probably got dust in them; but it's my bet you'll be all right, when there's light to see by. I were lucky – I had me face against you when we fell. Can you move your legs?"

Diverted, her trembling lessened, and she obediently bent her legs slightly and wiggled her feet. He felt the movement, when she arched her back. "All of me seems to work," she announced with a tremulous laugh. "I can't turn me head, though, 'cos me hair's caught under summat."

They lay quiet for a minute, while the dust thinned. Then she asked pitifully, "How long will it take 'em to get us out, Dickie?"

He sighed – carefully, so that he did not commence to cough again. He had been thinking about this and was privately convinced that it would be a miracle if they

135

were ever found. While Emmie had been unconscious, he had lain over her, dazed by the fall, his mind trying to grapple with the mystery of where they were.

They had been in the light well, lying on the ground, against the wall of the canteen under the little kitchen window. They must, he argued, have fallen straight through a fissure opened up by the bomb explosion. Yet, could they fall though a solid yard? He had definitely fallen through open space – he would remember the sensation until the end of his days.

The answer seemed to be that they lay in some old cellar under the cobbled yard. And who would dream of looking for them there? Only the people in the shelter knew that he and Emmie had gone into the yard, and judging by the fearful groans and shrieks with which his ears had been tortured for a moment or two after the bomb fell, those in the shelter were either dead or dying.

If all the buildings had come down, there could be sixty feet or more of debris above them. This had to be the end. And yet in him, bruised and scared as he was, lay a tremendous passion to live.

"How long, Dickie?"

"Dunno." The dust was settling now and it was much easier to breath, but delayed shock caught up with him and he fainted. Emmie felt the body stuffed in beside her relax and she thought he had died. She poked him with her elbow. He did not respond. "Dick! Oh, Dickie!"

Total fear engulfed her again and she began to scream helplessly, rendered almost insane with fright. She gibbered at him, as she tried to reach his face and finally succeeded in running one hand over it. Then she felt his chest heave slightly. She quietened and it seemed as if he were sleeping, and indeed he did pass into a light slumber.

She lay sobbing softly and between the sobs prayers tumbled from her lips. Promises to lead an immaculate life if only God would get her out of the tomb in which she lay came almost incoherently forth, as she tried to make a pact with the Almighty.

"I'll never hate Gwen no more. I'll help her all I can. She can have the bloody furniture. Oh, Jesus, hear me. What will Robbie do if I die? He's been so lonely for lack of a wife, oh, God. Have pity on him, if not on me. I know I'm as wicked a piece as ever was made, but I'll never miss chapel again, I won't. God have pity on me."

Deckie Dick became gradually aware of this litany, as he awoke and his mind began to clear. He was himself afraid of death, particularly a painful death. How would the Grim Reaper strike? Would the debris shift, to slide down and crush them? Would they die of thirst? Or starve like rats? Or, worse still, be eaten by rats before they had a chance to starve?

There was an increasing smell of escaping gas, faint but distinct. Deckie Dick also addressed his prayers to whatever Gods might be to let the gas thicken and engulf them. It would be a comparatively quick death; he had thought of sticking his head in the gas oven after his wife had died. With one son, Georgie, killed at Dunkirk and the other one, Billie, long since emigrated to the States, there was no one left to care about him. Now he wished, prayed, that this quick death might be granted to him and to the sweet woman lying next to him. Selflessly, he begged that there be at least sufficient concentration of gas to render her unconscious, so that she never knew what hit her, even if it was not sufficient to snuff out a tough old devil like himself.

v

Conor staggered into his crowded post, and Glynis Hughes looked up from tending a stout woman with a knifelike pain in her chest. The woman was nearly purple in the face and Glynis had been trying to keep her from going into hysterics, until one of the First Aid men, who had been called from the Dwellings, arrived with some more nitro-glycerine. The man followed Conor in, pushed him aside and plunged through the crowded room. Glynis snatched a spoon from a used teacup and handed it to him. She held the struggling woman, while he forced the life-saving liquid down her throat. In seconds, the pain abated, and Glynis thankfully left her to the care of the new arrival, while she pushed her way over to Conor, who stood like a zombie amid the crowd, his eyes half closed with fatigue. He was covered with grey-white dust, except across his knees and stomach, where his unform and the dust were stained dark red. Around him, the room hummed with voices, through which cut the sound of the telephonist relaying details of casualties and damage as they were brought to her. The line had been broken during the night and, despite a quick repair, the telephonist was having difficulty, as she laboured in a high-pitched voice to overcome the crackling of the line.

"Got a cup o' tea, Glynis?" his voice grated, as she reached him.

She eased her little buttocks past the back of the

138

telephonist's chair and laid a hand on his arm. "Sure. I'll get you one. But – but first I got to tell you somethin'. Come out in the street a mo'; it's quieter."

How am I going to do it? she worried. He always teased about his old woman, but he was fond of her for certain. And she was a kind woman, me mam always said. Dumbly, Conor allowed himself to be ushered into the street and a little away from the gossips by the door. Glynis turned and looked up at him compassionately. "Conor," she whispered.

"Is it one of the kids?" he asked, suddenly alert.

"No, Conor. It's Ellen." She grasped one of his hands hanging limply by his side. "She's gone, Conor. Mr Baker came earlier. Said she got a piece of shrapnel straight to her heart. 'Twas instant. She didn't suffer. I'm so sorry, Conor." She was trying not to cry, as he stared unbelievingly down at her. "The kids are all right. Your next-door neighbour – Mrs Thomas, isn't it – she's got them all and is taking care of them. The house is OK, too."

Conor licked his dry lips. "Where's Ellen?"

"She's laid out in the church hall – along with the others from The Dwellings. Monty got her picked up from the house real quick, in case your kids went in there. He's still here, if you want to pop over and see her."

His hand clenched hers tightly and the weary eyes closed. "I'm accursed," he said bitterly. "Accursed."

Glynis shivered. "Don't say that."

"First we lose everything we got, and nearly little Rube as well. And now Ellen."

"Go and see her," urged Glynis, a little desperately. "Father O'Dwyer'll be there, no doubt, to talk to."

"And what good will that do, to me or to him? And what good can I do for Ellen — Ellen!" He almost shouted and then his voice broke.

"You have to arrange her funeral — I'm sorry to say it."

He looked round him, like an animal trying to escape when cornered, then back at the tearful woman still holding his hand. "Glynis, down behind the filing cabinet in the post there's some whiskey — there's half a dozen bottles and more in the cellar. But don't say nothin'. Just get one out for me."

She smiled through her tears. So he did indeed smuggle whiskey. "To be sure," she said. "Trust me. We'll have a hot cup of tea with a good swig in it. You come back in, lad, and sit down a minute."

When she returned to him with a steaming cup of tea smelling strongly of whiskey, he was seated on a wooden chair, his face in his hands, and was weeping. Opposite him a middle-aged man, wrapped in a blanket, his bare feet sticking out from under it, sniffed and caught the odour of the spirit. Out of the corner of her eyes, Glynis saw the tired eyes light up. "I'll bring you a cup — exactly the same," she promised. "In a minute."

She put the cup and saucer into Conor's hand and then put an arm over his shoulder. He turned to her and hid his face against her breast. The tea slopped into the saucer. "I'm damned, Glynis," he mumbled. "Why Ellen? She never done anything wicked in her life!"

"I don't know," she replied sadly, and patted and stroked him, as if she were comforting one of her children.

When Gwen heard the knock on the front door, she thought it was David returning and that he had mislaid his key. She flew down the stairs clad only in her long, white nightgown and thankfully swung open the door.

She did not recognise for a moment the anguished man on the door step. Then a familiar Irish voice, with an unaccustomed wheeze in it, greeted her politely. "Mornin', Mrs Thomas. I'm told you kindly took me kids in?"

In the interests of modesty, she wrapped the cotton folds of her nightgown more tightly round her. Then she said, "Yes, indeed, Mr Donnelly. They're here. I think they're still asleep."

Without being invited, he stepped into the highly polished hall. Gwen's lips tightened, when he failed to wipe his feet on the doormat, a new one with the word *Welcome* knotted into it. He brought with him a strong smell of whiskey – and raw meat, was it? She shivered as she shut the door quickly behind him.

He looked uneasily round the hall and then sighed. "Do they know?" he asked her bluntly.

"No. Come in here for a minute." She ushered him into the small sitting room, and nearly cried out at the sight of her biggest aspidistra lying smashed in a pile of earth on her new red, imitation Belgian carpet, a carpet which had only two more payments to be made on it before it was entirely hers. Despite the breeze coming through the glassless windows, the room smelled cold and dank from disuse. Both the cretonne curtains and the blackout were in shreds. Gwen felt, in sudden rage, that she could happily strangle a German with her bare hands.

"What happened?" Conor almost snapped at her, as he turned to her.

A little frightened of the tight, frozen look of the filthy, tear-stained face in front of her, she stuttered an explanation. "Patrick knows," she finished up. "He's asleep on the sofa in the other room."

"I'll have to tell 'em, Mrs Thomas." He looked at her imploringly, hoping she would do it. But she was on the defensive now. There was a limit, she told herself. Enough that she had had these dreadful children thrust upon her. She couldn't.

"What if I get Patrick in here, and you talk to him?" she suggested.

He nodded, and turned to look out of the devastated window, while she gathered her nightgown even more tightly round her and went to get the boy.

"No!" she exclaimed in genuine horror, as she looked down at Ruby and Patrick tightly intertwined under the blankets on the sofa. She bent down and tapped Ruby on the shoulder. The girl woke with a jump. "Your father's here," she announced frigidly. "He wants to see Patrick in the sitting room. You stay here, miss." She would deal with their shocking indecency afterwards. Brother and sister sleeping together! She was scandalized.

Hardly comprehending what she had said, the two children looked up at their outraged hostess. Patrick yawned and then, without a word, he swung himself off the sofa and lurched unsteadily out of the room. Mrs Thomas pursed her lips and stared down at Ruby. Ruby slowly laid her head back down on the cushion she had shared with Patrick. She began to cry helplessly.

Gwen turned towards the fireplace and rolled back the hearthrug, preparatory to making the fire. "I should think so, too," she muttered angrily. "Such behaviour I never did see."

Yesterday, Patrick would have sworn that he hated his father. But now the object of his jealousy was dead and his father suddenly seemed a pillar of strength. He stumbled towards him and Conor held him, while they both wept heartily. Finally, Patrick snuffled, "Rube knows."

In the living room, Gwen put down her poker. She was suddenly cold. without a word to the weeping girl, she ran quickly upstairs to get her dressing-gown.

Immediately she vanished, Ruby sat up, untangled herself from the blankets and ran, barefoot, into the sitting room and flung herself into her father's arms.

With an arm round each of his children and tears smudging his dusty face, Conor asked them not to tell the little ones that their mother was dead. "Tell 'em she's in hospital being mended," he suggested. "Better they know when your gran comes down from Walton. I tried to phone the post there, so as to get hold of her quick – it were dead – so I wrote to her, but with it being Sunday today, she won't get it till tomorrer." Gran was his own mother. Ellen's mother lived in Dublin – and he realised suddenly that he must write to her as well.

"You all stay with Mrs Thomas, till I can get home. And you help her, Rube."

Ruby agreed sulkily that she would help her. "Pat, you feed me cocks – and beg a few scraps from Mrs Thomas for Sarge." The boy sniffed lachrymosely and

143

nodded agreement. He could hear Gwen in the next room raking out the fireplace. Even the sound of the poker seemed angry.

Gwen was just putting a match to the paper of the newly laid fire, when Conor entered, Ruby hanging on to his arm. Patrick followed, his face stony.

Conor loosed himself from his daughter and bent down to seize one of Gwen's coal-blackened hands and shake it hard. His breath stank of whiskey; still kneeling, she recoiled from him.

"It's proper kind of you to take in me kids, Mrs Thomas. I'll not forget it. Mr Baker said you would keep them for a while. By the looks of things, I won't be home until tomorrer – at least. It's terrible up at The Dwellings. You never saw anything like it. Keep the kids away – it's no sight for them. I've written to their gran, but with everything being upset in the town she probably won't get the letter till tomorrer afternoon at earliest." He paused for breath and looked at her anxiously.

"I – but – I ..." she began, a fearful sinking feeling in her stomach.

He burst into speech again. "I tried to get the wardens' post up there on the phone. Can't get through to anybody." He seemed to take it for granted that she would keep the children with her, and went on, "We won't tell the little ones their mam is gone, till their granny comes to comfort 'em." He took a turn about the room, while Gwen watched him, speechless for once. "You can say she's in hospital, doing fine, soon be home, like."

She opened her mouth, to make an excuse for not keeping the children, but he deflected her by asking, "Where's your hubby?"

"Still workin' out at Bootle. And our Emma isn't in yet."

Overwhelmed by his own troubles, Conor failed to realise that Emmie must have been in the thick of the air raid. He said mechanically, as he hugged Ruby again and turned towards the door, "She'll probably be in just now."

While the children saw their father out, Gwen leaned forward and mechanically struck another match to light the fire, which had failed to kindle. She sat on her heels, watching the flames creep through the newspaper and wondered what to do. There was not enough food in the house to feed everybody and little money in her purse to buy more. David would be furious if she exceeded her housekeeping money. Mechanically she gave the fireplace a quick whisk with a brass-handled hearth brush, and then continued to sit listening to the wood crackle, feeling exhausted, defeated.

Ruby watching her, hesitated in the doorway and then advanced diffidently. She put her arm shyly round Gwen and said, "Don't cry, Mrs Thomas. I'll help yez."

Startled, she turned in the curve of the child's arm. A little stiffly, she put her own arm round Ruby. "Well, thank you, Ruby." The girl smelled to high heaven. Hadn't her mother taught her to wash herself? Perhaps she hadn't been taught not to sleep with her brother, either, she meditated grimly. She scrambled to her feet. She *must* do something.

While Mari still slept, Ruby and Patrick were set to work, she to sweep up the remaining glass in the living room and he to tack some pieces of old lino culled from the cellar, over the gaping windows. The table was laid and a small helping of cornflakes put out for each child.

"And after breakfast, if you're going to be here overnight, everybody had better have a bath."

Both Ruby and Patrick were taken aback. They had never had a bath; only an occasional wash all over in the kitchen bowl; they were saved from having to reply by Nora and Brendy rushing down the stairs in a panic, having forgotten where they were. They surveyed the living room with popping eyes, broke into roars of tears and demanded to go home to Mam. Ruby mothered them both and soon they were shovelling cornflakes into their mouths, while they watched very suspiciously the preparation of the tin bath set in front of the fire.

Michael shrieked from upstairs and Ruby ran up to him. He had soaked the bed and was standing on it, holding the brass head rail. In the half darkness of the room, Ruby held him to her and told him Mam would be coming soon to fetch him. No amount of soft talk, however, would persuade him to eat cornflakes or even drink milk from a glass. He wanted his mother's breast.

Gwen surveyed him in harassed silence for a moment, as he sat on Ruby's knee kicking out in a furious paddywack. Finally she said wearily, "He'll eat when he's real hungry. Let him be for now. We might as well bath him first." She moved the dish of cornflakes away from Michael's flailing arms. "Do you have any clean nappies or pants for him at home? And any clean clothes for the other kids?"

"There's some," Ruby answered her doubtfully. "Me mam washed Thursday." She dreaded that Gwen might command her to go to fetch them. Her stomach churned at the idea of finding her mother lying so still in the hall.

Patrick came in from the kitchen, carrying a steaming bucket of water to tip into the tin bath. "I'll go and get 'em," he said heavily. "I got to feed the birds – and Sarge. They'll have taken Mam to hospital by now – won't they, Mrs Thomas?"

Gwen had forgotten about Ellen. She hesitated, and then said, "I think so, lad."

Mr Baker had remembered to let the dog out into the tiny back yard, and Sarge greeted Patrick ecstatically. He padded into the house behind the boy.

Patrick went straight to the front hall, almost hoping that his mother would be lying there, made comfortable by nurses, and that she would open her eyes and say she was fine, just waiting for the ambulance. But there was only the quilt from Ruby and Nora's bed piled against the wall. Slowly an all-consuming rage spread through him, that strangers had taken away his mother without his seeing her again. He kicked angrily at the quilt, and Sarge, who had been nosing round it, slunk back, tail between legs. He stamped his feet and then banged his fists against the wall, bent his head and hit that too against the hollow plaster. "Yer pack of sewer rats," he screamed at the anonymous ghosts who had come in the night to carry away his mother. He forgot about the clothing he was supposed to collect and ran through the house, up the stairs and down again, kicking open doors, screaming obscenities which echoed through the house, yelling what he would do to a German if he ever met one. He picked up some used cups from the kitchen table and slammed them on to the floor and crunched the broken pieces under his boots, until the fury of frustration waned and he stood sobbing helplessly in the deserted kitchen.

There an anxious Ruby found him. She put down on the floor an extraordinarily clean Michael, clad only in his jersey. The child was sucking his thumb, tears still wet on his face. He glanced round the kitchen, looking for his mother. Small sobs shook him from time to time and he stared in a dazed fashion at his big brother.

Ruby put her arms round Patrick. "It's no good, Pat. She's gone."

The boy pushed her away and turned his back on her. He mopped his eyes with the end of the woolly tie of his jersey.

"We have to find some clothes for Mrs Thomas."

"Damn her."

"Don't knock her, Pat. She's trying to help. We'd be in a right muddle without her – and no Dad either."

He turned a dark, passionate face on his sister. "I can't stand her. I'm not having no bath. I'm going to see what Dad's doin'."

With a huge sniff, he swung past her, opened the front door and slammed it after him.

Ruby stared after him, her whole body trembling with fear of the responsibility left to her, fear of offending Gwen, fear of not being able to cope with Michael, Nora and Brendy, fear of being terribly alone to face everything – perhaps yet another air raid that night.

vii

"It's quietened," Emmie pointed out. "It must be Sunday morning by now. We've been here ages, Dickie, and I'm so parched. Are you thirsty?" The voice was thin and quivery.

"Aye, I am. 'Could use a pint." He cleared his throat. "Yer know, there's a bit o' water here, somewhere. I can hear it trickling – faint, like."

"I know. It's not very far, but I can't move 'cos of me hair." Emmie's voice quavered and threatened hysterics again.

"There's a straight wall on t' other side of you, isn't there?"

"Yeah." She raised her arm up as far as she could reach, and winced with pain from bruises acquired in her fall. "There's enough space above me – I think – for me to sit up. She ran her fingers along the obstruction above her. "It feels as if there's a very big rough stone over us. It slopes down towards you, till it must touch you. If I could turn on me side, I could give you more room."

"Sardines in a bloody tin," he snorted. "Can you reach over your head to your hair where it's caught?"

"Mm. I've bin tryin' to pull some of it loose."

"I've got a penknife in me pocket. I doubt I can get it out, though. I've hurt me wrists, and me hands is as sore as hell."

"Oh, Dick! You never said you was hurt?"

"It's nought terrible. Could you reach in me right-hand keck pocket?" She felt him wriggle himself slightly upward, so that he was more level with her.

With her long, bony Lancashire fingers, she hunted feverishly down his side, stretching as far as she could. She touched his belt. "Lower," he instructed her. "Look, I'm goin' to ease meself a bit across you." She felt his head move across her shoulder till it lay against hers. He tried to ease the dead weight of his body over her arm. He grunted. "That's it. See if you can reach now."

The long fingers ran down his thigh, paused and then scrabbled at the pocket opening. "If you truly can't get it, I'll put me own hand in — but it's that tender, I don't want to."

"Hold still," she advised him. "I'll winch the pocket lining out." She giggled nervously. "You've got all sorts in here. I got your hanky out."

"Well, don't lose it. Put it where you can find it. We'll wipe our faces with it."

She obediently hauled it out and stuffed it down her chest.

Again the long, exploring fingers. He gritted his teeth; not with pain, but to control the sudden arousal which her warm nearness and her gentle fingers was exciting. The tendrils of hair against his cheek were having their effect, too. Many times, when he had seen Robert and Emmie walk out of the canteen with arms around each other, he had been pierced with envy and wondered what she would be like to bed. Now, however, crammed in a hell-hole which was likely to be their coffin, his desire for her was so strong that he longed passionately to roll back on top of her and have her.

She was his best friend's girl, he reminded himself forcefully, and with eyes screwed tight he kept himself rigidly still, until she almost shouted, "I got it. I got it."

"Good," he muttered, and took a large sighing breath and promptly sneezed.

She was panting with the effort she had made and began to cough again. When the paroxysm had passed, she cleared her throat, and said, "Afore I start sawing at me hair, I'm going to wipe your face with the hanky." She paused, and then added with a tremor in her voice, "Me own old dial is too sore. I'm bleeding a bit, I think."

150

"Ta." Poor kid, he thought. If her face is ruined, how'll she endure life, even if we are rescued?

She could feel his breath on her cheek. "Is *your* face hurtin' at all, afore I touch you?"

"No, Em. I think I were pressed against you when we fell."

His face was carefully wiped. She spat on a corner of the hanky and ran it clumsily around his eyelids. God, how he wanted her. She was surprised, yet pleased, when a kiss was planted on her cheek. She pushed the hanky back down the front of her blouse. "Now," she said almost cheerfully. "I'm goin' to start chopping. Proper sight I'll be when I'm finished." It was comforting to feel the man's warmth against her, especially when a particularly loud crash made the whole structure above them vibrate, and small rushes of debris slithered down on them.

The smell of gas had gone, Dick realised. The firemen must have managed to turn off the main. So much for that. He did not know whether to feel relief or disappointment. Willy-nilly, as shock had receded and been replaced by more mundane yearnings, a faint hope crept into him, that maybe the bomb that hit the canteen was not engraved with his and Emmie's names, that they might, by some miracle, be found.

Whimpers came from the girl next to him, as she tugged and cut hair by hair. She sighed and stopped work, to rest herself for a moment. Then she said without preamble, "We must have fallen into somebody's cellar – right under the yard, 'cos we was still outside – and I fell and slid quite a ways." Her voice was mournful. "I ache all over from it. Who'd build a cellar under a yard?"

"Plenty o' people, not too many years ago – about a coupla hundred, maybe. For keeping smuggled goods in – or privateers hiding their loot."

"They would? How'd they bring the stuff in?"

"A hidden door from the cellar under the building – where the shelter was, like."

"There weren't no back door out of that shelter."

"Could've been bricked up when they built the present building."

She sighed, and recommended the cutting of her hair. If she could get her head free, perhaps she could move enough to find the water that trickled so maddeningly close to her. As they lay at present, Dick could not move much either.

viii

Though the raid was over, and to Emmie, deep in her prison, the din seemed less, the noise outside from the roaring fires was sufficient to make everyone converse in shouts.

With shoulders hunched and bodies bent close to their jetting hoses, firemen had managed to advance a little into the raging inferno of South Castle Street, at the back of Paradise Street. Then the water pressure fell to a trickle and they had to beat a hasty retreat. Petrol in a pump caught fire and it blew apart. Dispirited men watched helplessly as, fanned by a light breeze, the flames began to eat their way towards Paradise Street. Wandering wisps of smoke worked their way through the wreckage. Neither Emmie nor Dick said anything, as they lay rigid with fear in the face of this new menace.

The building in which the canteen had been housed had blown outwards across the street. It effectively blocked the movement of traffic, already in difficulties because of the bomb hole further down, in which Post Office engineers struggled to restore some kind of telephone service for the authorities.

A gang of Army Pioneers, aided by volunteers, both civilians and servicemen, inched their way down the centre of Paradise Street, shovelling smaller rubble into wicker skips; larger pieces were hauled to one side. "For Christ's sake, why don't they bring in some cranes?" groaned a man in blue mechanic's overalls, as he heaved and shoved in company with a German Jewish pioneer. They turned to move a huge metal desk which had lain upside down under the girder they had just shifted. "Jesus!" the mechanic exclaimed, as he stooped to get a grip on it. With all his strength he heaved and rolled it on to its side – and looked down in horror at what had once been little Dolly, the firewatcher.

Her uniform had been blown off her. Terribly crushed, her entrails spread out, only the long gleaming hair indicated that there lay someone who had been soft and pretty.

The Pioneer looked down at her in silent pity, while the less hardened civilian shouted, "Curse them, curse them!" beside himself with horror. He bent down and gathered the frail, sticky remains up as best he could and took them to the pavement. There was nothing to cover her with. Soon, he knew, somebody would come along with a bag to put her in. Weeping, savage with rage, he went back to work.

Help *was* coming. Through moonlit lanes and narrow streets snaked a stream of fire engines and ambulances, water tankers, kitchen lorries, mobile canteens and vans of food. Rescue parties, including miners and demolition experts, spent an uncomfortable night crammed into trains as they converged on Liverpool. Through broken roads, spanking clean American soldiers manoeuvred bulldozers and dump trucks, and great shovels, also mounted on caterpillar tractors, bigger than anything most Britons had seen before. They would eat into the choked thoroughfares and make a path for other vehicles.

The looters came gaily from the suburbs and the countryside, to rob those who had already lost so much.

ix

An unexploded land-mine, sitting quietly at the back of a deserted insurance office, suddenly blew up and the ear-splitting bang shook Emmie's and Dick's tiny refuge. It shook not only the debris above them, but the ground on which they lay, like some huge earthquake. In terror, they clutched each other, their heads buried into each other's shoulders, to avoid the dust which rose once more around them. Bits and pieces rattled and fell above them. The great stone over their heads held, however, though the beam which was holding down Emmie's hair shifted slightly and the remaining strands of her hair were freed.

"My God!" Dickie's teeth were chattering helplessly, as the bang was followed by a series of rumbles, gradually dying away into quiet.

Ears pricked, they waited for the next onslaught, but there was only the creaking and shifting of the ruins and the occasional splash of water. Very dimly, they also could hear what might have been slow traffic and, at times, felt the faint vibration of it.

As the dust settled again, Dickie muttered to a whimpering Emmie, "It *has* to be morning – that bang were too big for a bomb – it were something special. Come on, luv. Now's the time to feel around for a stone and bang on that wall by you, so a rescuer knows where to look."

Emmie stirred and half sat up. Dickie exclaimed at her sudden movement.

"Me hair came free in the last shake-up." She laughed tremulously and felt round for a likely stone.

For nearly half an hour, they banged steadily, to no purpose. During that time they had both, shamefacedly, to urinate and now lay in wet clothes.

As they rested, feeling surprisingly weak, Emmie said, "David – me brother – 'll be out lookin' for me. What about your folks?"

Dickie explained that he had nobody and that this was his weekend off from his duties as night-watchman at a seed warehouse. "They'll wonder where I am come Monday, though, when I don't turn up for work."

"Gwen – that's Dave's wife – she won't bother. She hates my guts. Be glad to see me dead, I truly think. All she cares about is her house. If you breathe out, she'll dust all round you."

Dick laughed. "She can't be that bad."

"She is," insisted Emmie. "Dave's proper patient with her. It'll be him as comes to find us."

"The wardens and the Rescue Squads is good at finding buried victims," Dick replied, to reinforce her hope of help.

155

David was, however, sound asleep on a bunk made of chicken wire in a street shelter in Bootle. He had worked until the siren went, on repairing water pipes in narrow, badly damaged streets, while housewives and children hung round him, waiting for the taps, or at least the fire hydrants, to start gushing again. They also had no gas with which to cook, and often torn chimneys made it impossible to build a fire in a grate. Once water was restored, a good many kettles got boiled in the back yard on a fire made from splintered beams. In most cases their tiny stores of food were ruined, tins laced by slivers of glass, the contents of cupboard blown into pieces and lost in the general mess of broken plaster.

On Sunday morning, fed by a grateful housewife, David and his mate, Arthur, continued to work, laying new water pipes. Two streets away, another gas main sent a scarifying sheet of flame into the sky, threatening to engulf the slums around them in fire.

A little soothed by the thought that David would be seeking her, Emmie said to Dick, "You'd better have your knife back afore I lose it in the dark."

He fumbled round until he found her hand and the knife. As he slipped it into his shirt pocket, he felt her begin to sit up again.

"My God! Me poor back," she groaned, as the stiffened muscles were stretched.

"Now watch it," Dick warned. His voice sounded muffled, the words coming reluctantly from a parched throat. "Move carefully. If you touch something solid, don't push it or we'll have an avalanche down on us."

"OK." If she could stop shivering, she thought, she would be less clumsy. The shivering would not stop, however. As she sat up, it became a wild shaking, her teeth chattering uncontrollably.

Dick heard her wincing, and the shuffle of her skirts against the loosened earth, as she finally got herself seated upright. Instinctively, she turned towards him, to bend forward and touch him. "Ow!" she squeaked, as she hit her head on the sloping stonework over him. When she rubbed her scraped forehead, it hurt much more than she had expected; there was a trickle, which might have been blood, down over one eyelid, and she whimpered slightly as she carefully wiped it away with a shaky finger.

"Steady on, girl."

"Suppose I move too far away and I can't find you again?" she croaked.

"Na," he assured her. "We're like a pair o' mackerels in a tin – waitin' for the tin-opener."

Her shaky laugh was close to being a sob.

She heard Dickie sigh with relief as the pressure of her body on him was eased when she moved. Very carefully she tucked her feet under herself and then kneeled up. She promptly hit her head again and sat back dizzily until the throbbing stopped. In a wild hope that there might be an aperture through which they might creep to greater safety, she rapidly ran her hands up and down and along the wall beside her. Her spirits fell, when she found that the huge rough-hewn stones of the wall met tightly with the sloping slab which roofed them over. There was enough height on the wall side for them to sit up, if they kept their heads bent, and she reported this to Dick.

"That'll be a relief," he replied. "I'll stay put till you've felt right round."

She crawled with difficulty a foot or two along the wall, until, where her feet had rested, her exploring fingers found what felt like a metal girder sloping the opposite way to the stone above her. She tried to reach over it, but the way was blocked with rubble; she managed, however, to slip her hand under it and work her fingers through a pile of cobblestones and plaster. As she eased her hand carefully in, there was a loud creak and dust began to rise.

"For God's sake!" Dick's voice held panic.

She snatched her hand back under their sheltering slab. "I'm doing my best," she said crossly, and then sneezed. The sound was answered by another small rattle of debris from the same direction. She stayed frozen until the last small piece seemed to have dropped. Then she voiced the need of both of them. "I wonder where the water's running?"

"Let's listen hard."

The sound indubitably came from somewhere beyond the iron girder.

She burst into tears.

"I'm comin' up beside you, Em. Just sit still. Steady as you go, there's a girl."

He wriggled out of his narrow niche, his shoulders aching sharply, the rest of his bruised body complaining bitterly. Guided by her whimpering, he hauled himself alongside her. He sat, panting and dizzy half leaning against her, and then he straightened up. "Phew, that's better." He listened again, and then said, "There's water there all right. May be from the pipes leading to the canteen taps."

Emmie sniffed. "Doesn't matter where it's from. It's on the other side of a bloody great girder, and the

158

girder's too big to either climb under or over. Even if you could, there's a lot o' smallish bits very loose there." she tried to still her chattering teeth, and then quavered, "I don't know what we did to deserve this. We're not wicked."

Dick gave a rattling laugh. In the pitch-darkness, he tried to visualise the tiny space in which they found themselves. Then he said ruefully, "War's like the weather; it falls on the good and the bad alike. Only them what starts it takes care to be well away from it." Then, with determined cheerfulness, he went on, "Never mind that. First, I'm going to move forward a bit, so you can lie along this big wall. You lie on your stummick, and very, very slowly slip your hand under the girder again and work your fingers into whatever's there. See if you can feel wet. It'll be easier for you to do than me — 'cos o' me weight, like. I'm plain fat."

"Right." Her voice was a little firmer. After a tight squeezing past each other, she managed to do as he had suggested, and she worked her arm further and further under the girder until part of her shoulder lay under the unyielding metal. It was all bone dry.

With her arm still stretched into the rubble, she lay and listened carefully. "It's no more'n a foot beyond, I'm sure," she wailed in despair.

"Not to worry," Dick wheezed. "It might make a puddle in time and we'll be able to reach it. Have you still got me hanky?"

"Yes. Down me chest."

"Good. If it makes a puddle we can reach, we'll get at it by soaking the hanky in it."

She remained prone for a moment, while she mentally savoured the joy of cold water. Then she cautiously withdrew her arm and heaved herself round until she could sit up.

"Eh, I'm that sore, and you must be, too," her tremulous voice came out of the darkness. "Why don't they come? It's been pretty quiet for a while now. It has to be morning. Surely they'll be lookin' for us?"

"As soon as you hear anything that sounds like them coming, we'll shout as hard as we can, so they know we're here. And we'll bang with the stones again."

"T' warden what come to the canteen counted us all. He'll tell the rescue men how many people to look for."

"Aye, he will."

Outside in the street, the Pioneers carefully consigned the warden to the mortuary and, with him, the remains of the police constable, who would at least have known there were people sheltering in the canteen basement.

Further down the street, in a bomb crater, a newly bathed and clean-overalled Post Office Telephones engineer relieved his exhausted colleague. Elsewhere, linesmen continued to string wires from anything they could hang them on, in an effort to re-establish communications within the city.

As less fatigued aid arrived from other towns, a mood of ebullience spread amongst the toilers. This was the end of this run of raids, they told each other. Everybody would be able to go to bed tonight and sleep it off, ready for work on Monday.

Emmie found Dick's hand and held it, as she dozed. Sometimes a very distant rumble shook their tiny lair; it sounded like big lorries moving, a promise of rescue, and they were comforted.

Without warning, there was an enormous roar, a detonation greater than any previous one, and the whole ruin in which they lay shivered and groaned. Loud cracks overhead made Emmie scream. She flung herself against Dick; in equal terror, he turned and clung to her. Again, a tremendous dust enveloped them. Instinctively, they ducked their faces into each other's shoulder, cowering together as they nearly choked.

The pandemonium died away to a rumble, only to be followed immediately by a whole series of explosions which shook their precarious shelter. Almost directly overhead they could hear the fall of masonry followed by the lesser sound of smaller debris slithering like a hundred snakes down through the wreckage. The great piece of stonework above them shuddered.

A terrified rat scuttled across Emmie's lap, sending her into hysterics.

Despite the desperate efforts of its crew and the fire brigade, fire had finally reached the main hold of the *Marakand*. Surrounded by flames, dive bombed all night, firemen and crew had been unable to scuttle her, and now, under whatever cover they could find, they crouched defeated. A four-ton anchor, blasted into the air, fell into the engine-room of a hopper and sank it as well. Acres of dock and warehouse were mowed down by the tremendous blasts and the ever-encroaching fire. Only after seventy-four hours of almost continuous racket did a weird silence descend on the embers of a whole district.

"I never want to see anything like it again," Robbie muttered fervently to his deckhand friend, as their captain checked his sooty, worn-out crew. "I'll be thankful to go to sea again."

Fogged by fear, unable to produce even one more scream, Dick and Emmie lay tightly together, both breathing shallowly. Each time the torn building over them lurched, a fresh poof of dust would surround them and they would cough and splutter.

Outside, the late spring morning was made horrible by a blizzard of burned paper which blew about the city, getting into people's eyes, clinging to clothes and faces like black snowflakes. The burned records of innumerable enterprises flattened during the night had been caught by the wind and whirled out of every broken building. Up and up they went into the smoke haze, to descend again in a supernatural storm. Through the smoke, flames still licked greedily.

By noon the road outside the canteen was passable to a single line of traffic driving very carefully, and further efforts were being made to find the remainder of the firewatchers assumed to have been on duty with Dolly. The air raid warden on day shift and new police, all looking wondrously spruce, had come on duty, and a heated altercation broke out between a demolition squad foreman puttering along the edge of the debris, and the new warden.

"How was I supposed to know there was a canteen there? There weren't no warden around, nor a cop for that matter, on this street. Thought it was all offices – and as for firewatchers, I've only got one unaccounted for now."

"Well, there *was* a canteen here and it'd be open," replied the warden irritably, "and we'd better get weaving on it." By his accent the demolition foreman must be from Manchester, presumably one of the over three thousand men which the warden had heard were being sent to Liverpool. No wonder the man didn't know where anything was.

"How many people, do you reckon?" inquired the foreman resignedly.

"Could be as many as forty."

"Good God! Somebody should've told me." He scratched his crew-cut hair and put his helmet more comfortably on his head. "They didn't say nothin' in command post."

The warden raised a gloomy face from contemplation of the anonymous piles of wreckage round him. "The command post lost nearly the whole shift."

As he strode towards them, the police constable in charge of the area, looked bleary-eyed, despite a clean and tidy uniform. He had just arrived, to commence his shift, only to find a new command post being assembled and nobody very sure of what the situation was. "Looks as if Constable Wilson got it last night. We can't find him," he was told. Heavy-hearted, he had taken the first telephone call on the re-established line. Now he shouted towards the warden, "There's a phone inquiry about a Miss Piggott – serving in the Sailors' Canteen – do you know if that's bin tackled yet?"

"I only just coom on duty," replied the warden defensively. "And t' command post's only just bin replaced – pack of strangers. There weren't nobody in a fit state to tell nobody nothin'. Joe, here, he just coom from Manchester." He cocked a thumb towards the lugubrious foreman, who looked even more glum.

The constable's face went red with suppressed rage. Bloody fool, why didn't he use his common sense and show the new foreman? Poor Wilson and the command post couldn't help being dead.

"Get a bearing on where the entrance was," he ordered the warden through gritted teeth, "and explain to the foreman how it were laid out. I'll get you more help, and alert ambulance people. The entrance to the shelter underneath the canteen was to the left of the entrance from the street." He ran back to the newly reconstituted command post.

While the warden, like a questing terrier, trotted up and down the partially cleared street, the foreman assembled his squad and checked that they were equipped with shovels and crowbars – and skips to hold the rubbish they would have to remove.

The warmth of the fires, further over, was born towards them, making them sweat. The hiss of water hitting flame and the drum of pumps bewildered the warden. If it were only quiet enough to climb the rubble and listen; then they would stand a chance of hearing survivors tapping. There were other noises to add to the confusion: explosions from No. 2 Huskisson dock; detonations, as Lancashire mining engineers showed another demolition squad how to break a way through mountains of wreckage, without bringing an avalanche down on themselves; the lives of men with demolition experience were to be preserved at all costs – their peculiar skills were all too rare. In a nearby street, a huge bulldozer manned by American soldiers was slowly crunching its way through a blockage, and that also added to the racket.

"I've got it," shouted the warden triumphantly, as he rubbed one eye watering with a mot in it. "Opposite the stump of this lamp-post."

Huge and ponderous as the foreman was, he immediately began to climb the fall opposite the broken lamp standard, walking with surprising lightness, probing gently with his crowbar, before committing his team to the search. When he was satisfied that he understood the lay of the pile, he set his men to work. "Come on, lads. Quick – but careful – mind." His melancholy expression fell still further. "Doubt anybody's alive under that."

A portly gentleman in a business suit and bowler hat accosted the watching warden, "Excuse me. Can you tell me where the Sailors' Canteen is? My wife was on duty there last night, and she has not come home this morning. When I tried to telephone, I could not get through."

The warden looked up sharply and then bit his lip with tobacco-stained teeth. "Aye," he said slowly, with a sigh. "It were here. They're workin' on it now, as you can see."

The gentleman's ruddy complexion went glistening white. His grey, military moustache quivered; words would not come. Finally, he breathed, "I was afraid of that."

The warden caught his arm, concerned that he might collapse. "Sir! They could be safe in the shelter – it were a good stout cellar." The warden had not an iota of hope. But then, he told himself, you never knew what quirk of fate could save the life of someone. "What was – is – her name, sir?"

"Clara Robinson, Mrs Clara Robinson." The man was already out of his black jacket and folding it neatly. He laid it down by the lamp-post stump and placed his bowler hat on top of it. "Thank you," he said fairly steadily, as he got a grip on himself. Then he turned and picked his way over to a labourer clearing a path from the edge of the fall inwards. "Give me a shovel. I'll help you," he said between tight lips.

"Best stay back, sor," a middle-aged Irish navvy, working ahead of the other labourer, advised him. "It's dangerous." He lifted his pick again and swung it down on the obstruction before him.

"I *have* to do something," Alec Robinson said firmly. He undid his gold cufflinks and rolled up his shirt sleeves.

The foreman came carefully down the slope of the pile, placing each foot precisely so that he did not fall into the debris.

The warden shouted up to him, "T' cellar had a pavement light what led right into it."

"That'll save a lot." The foreman's face lifted slightly, as he redirected his men, to facilitate the unearthing of this narrow window of heavy glass framed in iron and set directly into the pavement to give some light to the cellar. If it had not been pounded into the ground, it could give the rescuers immediate access. Then he turned and sized up the blenched business man who was working his way towards him.

"You could clear some space at the edge of the pavement," he told him kindly. "Make a way through to where the road has been cleared. We'll need a bit of space to lay 'em down, maybe, when we bring 'em out." He saw Alec Robinson's eyes widen with horror, and added hastily, "They could be hurt." He turned to the labourer. "Find 'im a shovel."

Alec Robinson thankfully took the proffered shovel and bent to the task, his heart heavy. An ambulance was already nosing its way cautiously along the street, followed closely by a fire pump. A wobbly stream of water was directed at the ruins further back, to damp them down and possibly contain the fire raging behind them, until the rescuers had finished their work. The stream was weak because of fractured mains, and the turbulence in the air caused by the fires themselves blew much of the water back on to the firemen and the rescuers. Still, they persisted.

While the workmen picked their way in with meticulous care, para-medical personnel, black bags in hand, came at a shambling run along the littered pavement opposite.

They were too early, so, with tin hats pushed to the back of their heads, they lit cigarettes and stood gossiping about a new film one of them had seen.

In what seemed to have become their own private bomb crater, the clay-bespattered telephone engineers continued their patient splicing of lines.

When Alec Robinson paused to mop his forehead, he was approached by a tall cadaverous man dressed in the grey uniform of a chauffeur. The man took off his peaked cap, revealing a bald head across which a few wisps of white hair had been carefully plastered. "Sir, I'm looking for the Sailors' Canteen. I'm Higgins, sir. The mistress has not come home, and we – that is, Mrs. Fleming, the housekeeper, and me – thought I should come down on the bus, to see if she's all right – the car being mothballed for the duration, sir." He turned and surveyed the appalling wreckage. "I trust I'm not looking at the canteen?"

Alec Robinson replied gruffly, "You are. Who is your mistress?"

"The Dowager Countess Mentmore. She's a volunteer."

A minute later, a chauffeur's cap and jacket were carefully laid by Mr Robinson's bowler hat and black jacket, and the demolition foreman had to find work for another volunteer.

The rescuers worked like moles, shifting obstructing masonry, splintered woodwork, pieces of filing cabinets and desks, a slippery cascade of law books, a huge Victorian lavatory, all interlaced with electric wires which might still be live, and miles of water pipes and gas pipes. A lot of this was passed back and piled on the pavement. Stout pieces of timber, desk drawers, finely panelled oak doors, all were used by the labouring men as props in the twisting passageway they were making. Every time there was a further explosion from No. 2 Huskisson this perilous little entry was shaken by the blast, but still the men perservered.

x

That dreadful Sunday, as Emmie lay in Dick's arms, her mind wandered. Both of them were drained by fear, thirsty beyond words and very hungry. It seemed to her that she was lying in Robbie's arms on the sandhills, behind the great sea wall at Meols, and they were talking of building a small cottage not too far from there, with a good slate roof and a parlour for best occasions.

She woke suddenly, not sure what had alerted her. Instead of the sunlight on the waving, coarse grasses of the sand hills, she faced a midnight blackness. She touched Dick's face with her hand, and he stirred and muttered hoarsely, "OK, luv?"

"Mm," she replied. She shivered; the wall felt cold against her back.

It felt wet! Her cotton blouse and petticoat were

sticking to her back. She must have sweated heavily or wet herself again. But there it was once more – a cold drop, a trickle down a strand of her torn hair and across her neck.

"Dickie," she gasped. "Wake up. There's water running down the wall behind me back. I can feel it."

Water? He swallowed and tried to answer her, but his dried lips would barely move. He felt clammily cold and he shivered.

"Sit up, Dick. I'm goin' to turn meself over."

"Can't sit up, 'cos of the slope over me," he managed to reply thickly. She was right, though. He could smell the odour of water on dust – and he could also smell an increased amount of smoke. His heart leapt with fresh apprehension. He eased himself away from Emmie, to help her turn.

Emmie was as excited as if they had already been rescued. Her mind cleared as, wild with hope, she knelt up and ran her hand along the wall. There *was* a steady dribble down it at one point. She put her sore cheek against it and then turned to lick it. Her tongue was promptly covered with grit, but it was moistened, none the less. She tried again and spat out the grit. "There's only a bit," she announced in a fractionally clearer voice. "I'm going to try and soak your hanky, though."

The water flowed faster, forming a small pool round her knees. The handkerchief was soon quite wet and she passed it to Dick to suck. He thankfully wiped his lips and put a corner in his mouth. He too had to spit out grit, but the relief was tremendous. He managed to move a little out of his niche and curve himself round Emmie as she knelt, to dip the hanky again into the wondrous little pool.

Emmie undid her skirt button and awkwardly hauled off her blouse, cursing roundly when she caught her elbow on the rough wall. She pressed the garment into the tiny stream. As it became wetter, she struggled to get out of her cotton petticoat in order to soak that also. "It'll make a little store of water," she puffed.

"I'm sorry I can't see you."

She blushed, and managed a small giggle. In the dark, she had not considered her nakedness. Thankfully, she pressed the sopping blouse to her throbbing face. She tried to wipe it gently but it hurt too much.

All around the great slab that protected them water began to drip, to a point where, no matter how they lay, they became wet, and they again huddled in each other's arms, to keep warmer, while they speculated on the source.

"Could be a leak from a pool which built up somewhere above us," offered Dick. "And now it's sifting down to us."

Their little lair shuddered, as a quick series of explosions from the *Marakand* shook it; a heavier splatter of droplets fell round them. Dick felt Emmie begin to tremble and he held her closer. Again he was tempted to take her, now that the air felt cleaner and he could breath properly. She wriggled more tightly to him and he knew that she wanted him. She turned on her back and he moved on top of her, so that there was space above them.

Despite the limited space, it was a wild lovemaking, as if both of them were young and filled with the frantic desire of youth. Every terrifying shift of the broken buildings above them; every great blast that numbed their ears as the deadly cargo of the *Marakand* wreaked havoc, though adding to their fear, also intensified their passion, until finally they lay exhausted and almost unbelievably at peace. They continued to caress each other, Emmie with a strange wonder that some one other than Robbie could make her feel so good. As she stroked him, she murmured incoherent endearments and he chuckled. "Not bad for an old man, eh?" he joked, and fell asleep.

He was awakened by her hoarse voice saying, "Dickie, I thought I heard something scrabbling about then."

"Eh, what?"

"Listen? Is that a voice?"

They held their breath; then without a further word felt round for the stones they had used to bang the wall with.

Frantic with hope, they both banged, and shrieked, "Help! Help! Help!"

Emmie's voice was much weaker than she realised, her throat swollen from her earlier screams, and Dick's was not much better; he realised ruefully that he had exhausted himself with Emmie; it was hard to get breath enough into his lungs to yell.

They paused to listen again. They could hear only the groans of the pile above them, as it slowly settled. Emmie began to cry.

xi

Gwen felt, that Sunday, that her life had been broken into, just like burglars broke into houses, that her house was as good as doorless and anybody could plunge in and out of it without so much as a by-your-leave. Never before had she had to extend a hand to anybody; she prided herself on minding her own business, on having the whitest doorstep in the street, the best-dressed daughter and the cleanest-looking husband – and, of course, getting her washing out on the line before any of her neighbours, on a Monday morning. Sunday was a day to meet one's friends at chapel and show off the hat one had retrimmed, and to anticipate with pleasure eating one's meat ration, slowly braised in the oven while one was at service.

And instead, she was surrounded by the most awful bunch of little horrors anybody could have wished on her. She surveyed them grimly, as they sat round the table at midday, eating like starving dogs. It was a pure miracle, she thought, that she had managed to provide a dinner at all; just like the story of the loaves and fishes. The Thomases' meat ration had been extended into a stew with the aid of a bag of potatoes, culled from Mrs Donnelly's kitchen, and three pennyworth of fades – discarded, shrivelled vegetables – from the corner shop. Nora, who had been entrusted with the message to the corner shop, had also brought two loaves of yesterday's bread and some milk – on credit. "The first time in me life I ever arst for anythin' on tick," moaned Gwen.

Patrick had been soundly clouted over the head by his father, for coming to view the ravaged Dwellings, and he now sat sulkily shovelling stew into his mouth, while Gwen slapped a couple of spoonfuls of it on to her own plate. She picked up her knife and fork and began to cut the tiny cube of meat, when suddenly she remembered.

"Emma!" she exclaimed, and put down her fork.

Ruby looked up from her task of feeding an unwilling

Michael with bits of bread sopped in a saucer of gravy. Mari who had got up only in time for the meal, asked with a small yawn, "Isn't she in bed?" She smiled across at Patrick, but he dropped his eyes and did not smile back.

"It were such a hectic morning, I clean forgot her. She never come home."

Mari stared at her incredulously, while Ruby stuttered, "Do you think she caught it last night?"

Mari licked her lips. "What about Daddy?"

"He'll be all right." Gwen's reply was automatic. Her husband was always all right, as dependable as the Liverpool one o'clock gun, which, before the war, had marked the time for the city. No one had told her of the carnage in Bootle – or, indeed, in the city itself; the wireless had merely reported a raid on a north-west town.

She sighed, as she looked round the table. Only Ruby and Mari were interested in Emma; the others continued to eat, Brendy happily pushing bits of vegetable into his mouth with his hand. "Really, Brendy," Gwen expostulated. "Use your spoon, you naughty boy." He took no notice and she leaned across the table and gave his hand a small slap; then she stuffed a spoon into it. He tried shovelling.

She turned to Patrick, as being the only older male present, and said agitatedly, "I'll save her some dinner, anyway. And you, when you've finished, run over and tell your dad she's missing. He'll know what to do. He'll ask about her for us."

Patrick nodded agreement. If he had a real message to deliver, surely he would be able to stay to watch the men at work on The Dwellings. He quickly ate the last

173

mouthful on his plate and half rose from the table.

"Have your pudding first," Gwen ordered. "A few more minutes ain't goin' to make no difference."

Pudding as well. For the first time that day, Patrick's spirits rose a little, and he ate eagerly the large helping of bread-and-butter pudding she put in front of him.

"Where did Miss Emmie go?" he inquired.

Gwen explained about her job in the Sailors' Canteen in Paradise Street and that she was on the evening shift. She ran her fingers through her greying red curls. She had been too busy to comb it and had not even washed her face.

"I'll take me dad's bike and tell 'im first; then I'll ride down to Paradise Street and see what's to do there." He looked excited at the prospect and gave Gwen the same beguiling, conspiratorial grin that had mesmerised Mari in the air raid shelter. Mari, seeing it, felt again the extraordinary sensation which his exploring fingers had introduced her to. She flushed and went slowly on with her dinner.

"I hope she's all right," Gwen said mechanically. "She might've gone over to see Robert Owen's mother." In her heart she felt that Emmie was a deliberate nuisance in not turning up for either breakfast or dinner. Serve her right if she'd got killed. Decent girls came straight home. And then there were all those merchant seamen hanging around the canteen – a lot of no-goods with only two ideas in their heads, drink and women.

Patrick could not find his father at The Dwellings because he had taken half an hour off to go to see the local undertaker about his wife's funeral. He reluctantly approached the constable in charge of the incident, who promised to put an inquiry about Emmie in motion immediately, and to let Mrs Thomas know as soon as he had news. The constable refused to allow him to go close to the ruins, so Patrick again mounted his father's rusty bike and sped away to join the sightseers in the town. At the top of Duke Street, he was stopped by a soldier with a rifle on his back, who wanted to know his business and promptly turned him back.

Patrick knew the town like a rabbit knows its warren. He gravely cycled round the corner out of sight, then dived down an alley and proceeded along back ways. He did not return for tea.

xii

Gwen gave the children a tea of bread and margarine and home made gooseberry jam and sent them out to play in the street. It was the first day in her married life that she had given barely a thought to the condition of her little house, except nearly to weep over the bed which Michael had wetted; it was now being dried out with the aid of three hot-water bottles. She sat with eyes closed, wishing passionately that David would return. He would know what to do about the Donnelly children – and Emma and the windows – and the fact that she was going to be over her housekeeping money.

She was sound asleep in the chair, mouth open, gently snoring, when Conor Donnelly, followed by Ruby, walked in through the open front door.

She awoke, startled to see an awful apparition standing before her on her rag rug. It was white with dust from head to foot, the face caked. Two red eyes glared out at her from under a battered tin hat; ominous brown stains marked the front of him. There was a faint smell about him as if of a butcher's shop, mixed with old sweat. A gap in the face was mouthing something about Emma.

Frightened, she jumped to her feet so quickly that she nearly knocked him down.

"It's me dad," explained Ruby simply.

Gwen forced herself into wakefulness. "Did you say Emma?" she asked. Then, without thinking of the effect on her fireside chair, immaculate in faded cretonne, she said, "My, Mr Donnelly, you look dreadful! Sit down. Would you like a cuppa tea? Have you had your tea?"

Conor flopped thankfully into the little chair and tried to smile. "Ta, I could use a drop."

"No trouble." To offer a cup of tea was a strict convention, but she surveyed him with dismay. Never in her life had she seen anyone look so dreadful. Even the chimney sweep at the end of a day's work – or the coalman – never looked as bad as that. For once her Methodist training surfaced, and she asked impetuously, "I got a bit o' dinner left. Why don't you wash your hands and face under the kitchen tap, while I make it hot for you?"

He had eaten nothing hot for forty-eight hours and he accepted eagerly.

It was amazing what a bit of hot food would do for a person, thought Gwen in gratified surprise, as she watched Conor polish off the dinner intended for Emma. Scuttling round to make the food ready, she had forgotten again about Emma, but now as he slurped at a cup of tea, she remembered and inquired if he had news.

He sighed. "Aye, I have, Mrs Thomas. The canteen's flat. They're digging into the shelter under it now."

"And Emma's in it?" Her heart bounced uncomfortably. It was one thing to wish a person dead or gone; quite another to probably have the wish granted so promptly.

"I suppose she's there. They're trying to finish the job afore it's dark – same as we bin doin' at The Dwellings."

"Do you know how things are in Bootle?"

Anxious not to scare her unnecessarily, since her husband was out there, he played down the shocking fate of Bootle.

"Me hubby didn't even come home for his dinner," Gwen remarked quite crossly. "Don't they know men have families to look after?"

Conor ignored the remark and pursued the question of Emmie. "Miss Thomas were engaged, weren't she?"

"Yes." Gwen was surprised that he knew. She had forgotten that the engagement of a woman of mature years would have been an interesting piece of gossip to be mulled over by the fire in the local public house.

"Is he at sea?"

"I doubt it – yet. They were loading at No. 2 Huskisson, according to Emma."

"What?"

Gwen jumped. "At Huskisson. Why?"

Conor told her the news, received over the post telephone, of the fearsome destruction wreaked by the exploding *Marakand*. "Most of the bangs you've been hearing today is from her," he finished up.

"Well, I can't say as I think much of him, to be truthful – but I wouldn't wish that on him." She had a sudden picture in her mind of the tall, well-built man, ruddy-faced and blue-eyed, and knew in her heart that she was deeply jealous of Emmie. Emmie was so content, so satisfied, as if part of the time she was moving in a dream. David had never made her glow like that. She felt a surge of longing go through her thin frame and she examined her nails carefully so that Conor would not read her feelings in her face.

Conor said heavily, as he got up from his chair, "I'll see if we can trace him. Robert Owen, deckhand, on the *Marakand*, wasn't it?"

She nodded absently.

MONDAY, 5 MAY 1941

Neither Emmie nor Dick admitted to each other an increasing hunger; hunger was something which had been with them, on and off, all their lives. At her brother's house, Emmie had for the first time enjoyed adequate meals, though Gwen was by no means generous in the portions she gave her. Now, however, she endured a clemming misery.

As they became wetter, the water which had been such a Godsend became a trial. Dick shivered constantly, teeth chattering, from the cold as well as from nervous strain.

Not only did they lie in puddles of water, but in their own urine and ordure, and the odour vied with the smell of smoke and wet plaster; the wisps of smoke saved them, however, from attacks by rats, the contemplation of which made both of them heave at times; the vermin with which Liverpool was infested retreated as the fires advanced.

At one point they thought they heard the scrape of metal on stone and then a distant shout. In response, they banged the wall with a stone and cried out again and again. The wall was as thick as a castle keep and if there was anyone there, the frantic cries went unheard.

In a sudden burst of fury, Emmie had said venomously, "If I ever get out of this fix, I'll go into munitions. I'll send them something to make *them* smart, I will."

"You can make good money at it," Dickie replied practically. "A lot more'n you could servin' in a cafe."

This idea had set her off on a laboured, barely audible description of what she would like to do after the war, if she had some savings. "I'd buy a nice little sweet and tobacconist's," she confided to Dick. "It'd give me some real independence – and summat to do while Robbie's at sea."

"He might like to swallow the anchor and help you."

"Nay," she insisted, with unexpected woodenness. "He can have 'is own job. This is for me. I never ever thought o' planning for meself afore this." She contemplated a hopeful future for a little while. Then she said, her voice cracked and broken, "You know, a lot of women get tired of being bossed all the time, but unless you got money you got to put up with it. I'm tired of it. I want to be free – and Robbie will benefit. We'll have more money for both of us. Go on holidays and suchlike."

Sporadically, they planned holidays and dreamed of sunny beaches, until an ache in Dickie's back became a piercing pain; his temperature started to rise and finally his speech to wander, until he was talking to Emmie as if she were one of his sons.

Emmie, too, began to feel light-headed, and the unbroken darkness robbed her of any knowledge of the passage of time. Unaware of the frantic battle being waged in No. 2 Huskisson, in which her beloved Robbie fought as hard as anyone, she concluded from the intermittent booms which shook the ground beneath her that it was night and a raid was taking place at a little distance from the town centre.

Just before midnight, and continuing well into Monday morning, enemy aircraft swept over the east coast, like a cloud of disturbed hornets, curved round over Liverpool Bay and followed the shining Mersey to their target.

The anti-aircraft guns had been reorganised during the day, to good effect, and a heavy barrage greeted the raiders, making it difficult to bomb accurately. Nevertheless, incendiary bombs deluged the city, and the haphazard scattering of high explosives brought out of bed at a run all those citizens brave enough to retire in the first place. People sleeping on the platforms of the underground railway forgot the hardness of their sleeping place and turned over thankfully, and those in air raid shelters or out in the fields beyond the city congratulated themselves on their forethought, miserable as they might be. The stunned victims of the earlier raids, now herded into schools and church halls, faced this further threat to their safety, and more than one such shelter became a bloody grave before morning.

Though night fighting was a new art, the pilots in their slow Defiants used all their ingenuity to defend the port. "Learnin' on t' job, like us," one auxiliary fireman remarked cynically, as he gazed upwards for a moment at the fireworks in the sky. A thin cheer went up from his battered brigade, when a Nazi airman was spotted bailing out and floating downwards, his parachute spread above him. "Hope he gets lynched," cried several savagely tired Liverpudlians; but he was picked up from the river the next morning, drowned, like so many of Liverpool's own men.

Ignoring the pandemonium and the danger, Rescue Squads still picked their way delicately through great heaps of what had once been a city. With the aid of shaded lamps or, infrequently, a floodlight, they peered and called and probed, with occasional success, while searchlights flicked like mad pendulums back and forth across the sky and malevolent pieces of flak flashed like javelins amid the rescuers.

Panting, trying to keep calm, Emmie held the head of a babbling Dick to her naked breast, clasping her arms tightly over him as she sought to protect him. As the hubbub continued, furious sexual desire engulfed her again. It boiled in her, an urgent, primitive need, and she murmured incoherently to him. Dick himself was aware only of a warm, comforting presence in a world of nightmare, as pneumonia took hold of him. His breath came in harsh rasps.

"Don't let him die, oh, God. Don't let him die," she implored, as she realised there would be no response from him. While the ear-splitting din round her increased, she began to believe that he was indeed dying; her self-control deserted her, her mind gave way and she shrieked like a rabbit in a snare.

ii

As she saw Conor out of the front door, on Sunday evening, Gwen managed to insert into his monologue the suggestion that the children might now return to their own home, since it was fairly certain, from experience in other raids, that the Germans had finished this onslaught. Shocked, Conor had turned back and vehemently begged her to keep them with her for one more night.

"Their nan should be here by tomorrer night," he assured her. "She'll stay a few days, though she's still got me dad to care for at home. Then Rube will have to manage for us – we'll hope the raids'll be finished by then."

When Gwen still demurred, he insisted, "I *can't* stay home with them tonight. They need every man they can get at The Dwellings. What would people say if I stayed home, I ask you?"

Because of what people might also say about her, Gwen reluctantly agreed to keep the youngsters.

She went slowly back indoors. In the yard, Conor's dog started to bark and then to whine. "Blast him," she muttered viciously. The kitchen door to the yard opened, and Patrick entered, the dog sidling after him. He looked white and strained and glanced at her uncertainly before dropping his eyes to the importuning dog and patting it.

He's scared, Gwen sensed. Frightened to death of something.

"What's up, lad?"

"I don't think anybody's alive down there," he burst out, his breath coming quickly, as if he had been running.

"Where?"

"Down Paradise – where your Emma was."

Gwen felt herself go cold. So the worst had happened. She had wished it and she was responsible. She wanted to be sick.

"It's somethin' terrible down there, missus. You should see the fires." His lips trembled. He had seen what he feared even grownups could not cope with and he was frightened, humbled. Dreadful Mrs Thomas looked suddenly like a pillar of strength; her basement steps a safe stronghold.

The gates of hell yawned before Gwen. If you wished

185

a person dead – and it happened as you wished – it was as good as murder. She gaped at the beaten child whose grubby hands clutched for support at the back of the chair. Then she said very slowly, "What you and I need is a cuppa tea." She tried to pull herself together, and added, "And I'll make you gooseberry jam butties to go with it." She walked unsteadily past him to the kitchen and he and the dog followed her forlornly.

Faintly from the street floated the voices of Ruby and some neighbouring little girls singing a skipping song. The thud of the rope stopped and a quarrel broke out, in which Nora's strident shrieks predominated. A few moment later, a flustered Ruby dragging a recalcitrant small sister interrupted the tea making, and from the staircase another voice chimed in, as Brendy, clad only in his vest, howled, "I want me mam. Where's Mam?" He came pattering into the kitchen, pushing his way past his sisters.

Gwen gulped and half closed her eyes. "Be quiet!" she cried exasperatedly. "Shut up, Nora." She bent down to catch Brendy, who threatened to exit through the back door in search of his mam. "Hey, you're supposed to be in bed, now."

Nora stopped her battle with Ruby and joined in with Brendy. She looked up resentfully at Ruby and cried, "Aye, where's me mam?" She pouted, and rubbed her arm where Ruby had slapped her.

Gwen snatched up Brendy and tried to soothe him. "Your mam'll be back soon," she told him, patting his back gently. "You know she's gone to hospital to be mended."

Though she heard both Patrick and Ruby catch their breath behind her, this was sufficient to reduce Brendy's

186

howl to a sob. "Where's she broken?" he asked with a trace of interest.

Gwen sighed. "She's got a cut – just there." She touched Brendy's protruding ribs. "The doctor'll sew it up – and then she'll get better and come home, I hope."

"Get away," Nora exclaimed in disbelief, her pout wiped off her face. "With a bloody needle?"

"Don't you use language like that round this house, miss," Gwen scolded. "Or I'll wash yer mouth out with soap." Nora bridled, her sly eyes peeping defiantly between the almost white lashes. Gwen went on, "For sure, they stitch cuts up with a needle – and white cotton."

"Well, I'll be buggered!" Nora's eyes opened wide with amazement. "They couldn't?"

Gwen put down Brendy, picked up Nora's hand and smacked it on the back. "I told you to mind your language, you little vixen."

Nora scowled and was silent.

Brendy pulled at Gwen's apron. "When'll she come?" he asked piteously.

"Soon, luvvie, soon. Now you come up to bed. You'll get cold down here."

After Gwen, Ruby and Patrick had shared a pot of tea and he had told them some of the details of the shambles in the town, including the information that the rescue squads were still digging for survivors, Gwen sat white and silent for a moment. Then she said heavily, "You'd better go and feed your dad's cockerels."

He went grudgingly into his own back yard and stood watching the birds in their separate cages pecking at the black market corn, as he sprinkled it in front of them. When he unthinkingly put his fingers on to the chicken

187

wire which held them in, one bird pecked him. He swore at it. The burst of anger brought him out of the lethargy into which he had sunk, and as he sucked his finger, he watched with interest a plane high in the sky. It climbed in the pearly atmosphere until he could hardly hear its engine, and slowly a great ambition rose in him, to fly himself, to be a bomber pilot and give the Germans what for. He looked at the closed back door, where his mother had been fond of leaning, her latest baby in her arms, to catch the sun and wait for him to come back from school. Tears welled up and with them a murderous desire for revenge, a boiling tide of feeling which stayed with him for years. "I'll teach 'em!" he cried, as tears of grief ran down his face.

iii

Gwen crawled into bed beside Mari. In the next bedroom Michael whimpered fretfully.

"I wish Ruby could shut that kid up," she fumed uselessly.

Mari stirred uneasily. "He's hungry, Ruby says. He wants his mam. She used to feed him from her breast. I seen her."

"Good Heavens! That's not decent. He's far too old for that."

"Ruby says that's why he wants his mam so bad."

Gwen cleared her throat, a little embarrassed. "Well, a little girl like you shouldn't be talkin' about such things." She turned over, and buried her head in her big feather pillow. Mari thought she had gone to sleep, but she said abruptly, "I'd better get him a titty-bottle from the chemist tomorrow." She sighed, and then went on, "Till I can teach him how to drink from a cup."

A resounding crash, an hour later, took the corner grocery shop, and the sunken-cheeked woman who kept, it straight into oblivion. Mother and daughter flew out of bed. Nora, Brendy and Michael were howling in unhappy unison with the air raid siren.

Ruby met them on the landing, with a bawling Michael in her arms. She was panting with terror, her big grey eyes nearly popping out of her head. Nora and Brendy crowded behind her.

"Downstairs, quick," ordered Gwen, as she struggled into her dressing-gown. "And you, Mari, take the candle – and don't drop grease on the stair carpet."

Patrick had opened the front door and was watching the Defiants darting in and out amid the searchlight beams. "For goodness' sake, come in," yelped Gwen in nervous concern. "That's how your mother caught it."

He shut the door reluctantly as the other children scampered through the living room to the kitchen and the cellar steps. Inspired, Gwen snatched her sweet ration out of the sideboard drawer as she went past, and what had threatened to be a weary, noisy gathering became suddenly happily quiet when she distributed toffees all round.

At half-past four on Monday morning, they went gratefully back to their beds.

At five o'clock, David was dropped at his door by a car intended to carry the walking wounded.

He staggered into his home and sank thankfully into the familiar depths of his easy chair. He leaned his head back and the pain in his chest surged again. To hunt for the matches and light the gas jet was out of the question;

189

he concentrated instead on trying to breathe. Finally, the spasm passed and he sat absolutely still, beads of perspiration coating his forehead, until he heard Gwen running down the stairs. She hurried in, tying her plaid dressing-gown round her, as she pattered across the linoleum. Patrick stirred but did not wake.

"Dave!" she exclaimed. "Am I ever glad to see you." She peered at him in the half light. "Golly, you look dirty. Have you had any tea?"

David felt as if he were floating along in a mist, everything distorted, nothing close to him. He breathed with effort, afraid to move much, lest the pain recommence. The staircase up to bed loomed as an impassable barrier. "I'd like a cuppa tea," he managed to reply. He closed his eyes, and the faintest smile broke the exhaustion of his face, as he envisaged the whole of Liverpool afloat on pots of tea.

Gwen quickly folded back the little hearthrug. "Aye, David, what a time I've had. I've got all the kids from next door here. Patrick's there." She gestured towards the sofa, half hidden in the gloom. "Poor Mrs Donnelly – struck down in her prime."

"Dead?"

Gwen was kneeling in front of the fireplace, quickly raking out the ashes and then stuffing balls of newspaper and pieces of firewood into the grate. She paused and turned a pinched, weary face towards him. "Saturday night."

As best he could, David tried to pay attention to the story of the children, the windows, the broken aspidistra bowl, the dog in the back yard and Emmie's absence. Finally, she said, "And last night the gas went off. I put a whole shillin' in the meter and nothin' happened."

David sat with his eyes closed. Emma! "What did you do about Emmie?"

"Told Mr Donnelly and he's inquiring."

He knew he could not go out himself to look for her, so he simply nodded and said, "You can draw a couple of quid from the Post Office Savings. Aye, I hope she's all right." After these garbled instructions, he allowed himself to rest.

He was hazily aware of her feeding a horde of children, correcting them sharply and dispatching them to school. He woke sufficiently to return a hearty kiss and a hug from his daughter, doing his best to appear merely tired. Gwen had handed him a cup of tea, but he sat with it on a little table beside him until it went cold.

When Ruby left him, Michael yelled and had to be held back from following her. As the front door slammed, he threw himself on to the floor and kicked and screamed, arms flailing.

David was thankful when the piercing howls became sobs and then the sobs were separated by silences, as the little boy discovered David staring at him. The blazing blue eyes closed and, thumb in mouth, he went to sleep on the hearthrug at David's feet.

Gwen had run upstairs to put on her clothes, and now she came down and said, "Thank goodness, that's over. He won't eat, 'cos his mother used to feed him herself. I'll get him a titty-bottle from the chemist when I go down the road." She turned to survey David. "Would you like some cornflakes for your brekkie? Or do you want to get washed first?"

"Nay," he replied slowly. "See if you can get the doctor to come. I keep getting a pain in me chest."

"Pain? Why didn't you tell me? You don't look well, that's for sure."

The detail of the cramp in his chest was laboriously explained to her, as she flung her coat over her flowered overall and crammed her beret over her errant curls. She half ran the quarter-mile to the doctor's house.

According to his troubled wife, the doctor had been out all night. She would send him over as soon as he returned.

Breathless, Gwen returned more slowly. She was sick with fear. Was it a heart attack? Or warning of a stroke? She must keep him quiet – and that meant keeping Michael quiet, as well. She'd pick up a bottle and teat from the chemist when she passed his shop, if he were open.

As she went to turn into the chemist's doorway – she could see him inside, though the "Closed" sign still hung on his door – she bumped into Mrs Hanlon, a big, florid woman, the wife of a docker who lived a few doors away. Mrs Hanlon was bubbling with the exciting news of the demise of the corner shop and its owner, which lay in the opposite direction to the doctor's house and had consequently not been seen by Gwen.

"And what you goin' to do, now Blackler's is burned down?" the woman asked, wrapping her black shawl more tightly round her and leaning forward to breath into Gwen's harassed face.

The news was a real shock to Gwen, and Mrs Hanlon seemed to expand and contract, like a balloon in process of being blown up. Blackler's gone – and with it, presumably, her wages. Gwen's heart sank.

"And Lewis's," went on Mrs Hanlon ruthlessly. "T' firewatchers must've been roasted alive."

Gwen felt as if the whole universe was crushing down on her. "I got to go to the chemist," she intervened desperately. "Mr Thomas is sick."

Mrs Hanlon ignored the interjection and prattled on happily about The Dwellings and the pile of bodies there.

Suddenly, with overwhelming passion, Gwen hated her. Was it really a Roman holiday to her? Didn't she realise that every bomb that fell was like a huge stone in a pool; the effect grew and grew, like ripples in a pool. Not only did it destroy homes; it upset completely the lives of everybody near. And for what? For what?

As the remorseless voice went on and she tried unsuccessfully to ease herself behind Mrs Hanlon in order to rattle on the chemist's door latch, she thought of Michael screaming for his lost mam, and she wanted to run home and take him in her arms and tell him everything would be all right – in a while, when the ripples ceased – and to put a hot poultice on David's chest and tell him the same.

The chemist opened his door and at his polite "Excuse me" Mrs Hanlon moved out of the entranceway. Gwen whirled behind her and left the woman standing open-mouthed.

iv

A frantic Monday for every city official, with one hospital out of commission and several others badly damaged; in Webster Road mortuary over half the bodies nameless; water in short supply; wavering sheets of flame still flaring upwards from burst gas mains; dangerous electric cables snaking over many a road and in and out of wrecked buildings; hordes of hungry and homeless people; and the centre of the city a mighty funeral pyre.

To those Liverpool housewives who still had a home, however, the main problem was that they could not do their washing. Monday was national washing day and on Tuesdays one did the ironing.

As Gwen hurried through her back yard, on her return from the chemist, she realised that even if the trickling kitchen tap provided enough water, she could not hang the washing out in the yard to dry. The air was filled with tiny bits of grit and burned paper – she had a piece in one eye and it was watering miserably. A sandlike film had formed on all her brightly polished window sills, and when she ran her finger along the clothes line as she passed, she found it thick with dust.

She paused for a second, her hand on the doorknob, to get her breath before entering the house, and looked down at the neat sealing-waxed parcel the chemist had made of a feeding-bottle and comforter. Then with shoulders bowed like an old woman, she opened the back door and went slowly in.

David lay on the sofa, asleep. His usually ruddy face was ashen and Gwen noticed with a pang that his two days' growth of beard was grey, not black. He was still in his overalls.

Michael snuffled gently on the hearthrug. He was awake, sucking his thumb as usual. He held the little, brass-handled hearth brush in his arms as if it were a teddy bear.

She ran upstairs to get a woollen shawl with which to

cover David and was immediately thrown into a towering rage when she discovered, in passing, that the drawers of the chest in Nora's and Brendy's room had been opened and the contents were scattered all over the floor, amid feathers from a burst pillow. "Blast them!" she cursed, nearly crying.

She had just tucked the shawl over David, who did not stir, when there was a polite knock at the front door. Expecting the doctor, she hastily took off her overall and smoothed down her skirt, before answering. She was still shaking with suppressed anger.

On the unwashed doorstep stood a nun. Gwen glared at the tiny elderly figure in a spotless white wimple and a shabby, but perfectly pressed, black dress. Little highly polished black boots peeped out from under the heavy skirt and a large rosary hung from her waist. Her hands were tucked into her big sleeves. The face in the stiffly starched frame was paper-white and lined like crumpled tissue. Two gentle grey eyes surveyed Gwen and showed faint amusement, as Gwen stepped hastily backwards as if to avoid contamination.

Assuming that the nun was begging, she asked rudely, "What do you want? We're Methodists. We don't give to Catholics." She started to close the door.

"I have come with regard to the Donnelly children. I am from their school." The voice was soft but authoritative and Gwen opened the door slightly again. "I wanted to inquire if you need help with them."

With a long sigh Gwen said, "Well, I'm managing." She bit her lower lip and, remembering her manners, asked, "Will you step in for a minute? The parlour is wrecked, but come in anyways."

The nun floated in after Gwen and surveyed the dying

aspidistra lying amid its earth and the broken shards of its pot in the middle of the red Belgian carpet, the linoleum nailed roughly across the windows, and the soot in the hearth.

Gwen hastily brushed broken plaster off a straight chair brought from her mother-in-law's house. "Sit down," she invited cautiously.

"Are *all* the children with you?" asked the visitor, seating herself.

"Yes." The word came in a little gasp, and suddenly Gwen was pouring out to another woman, a woman, not a nun, all her worries about Michael, her fears that she could not keep Patrick under control, about Ruby's little shoulders having to carry such a terrible load in the future, and about foul-mouthed Nora and Brendy. "Their gran's supposed to come today," she finished, pushing back her wild hair from the eye that was still watering. "And me husband come back this morning with a pain in his chest. He's asleep back there. We're waiting for the doctor now."

"I understand. I can quite understand your concern." Gwen had been standing in front of her, and now the sister caught her hand and patted it. "I'll have some additional clothing sent over to you — and a box of groceries — you could pass them on to their grandmother – if she arrives safely."

Afterwards, Gwen warmed some milk and put it into the new feeding-bottle. How strange it was. Under all that black cloth lay the kindest of human beings. She said to Michael, who was sitting on the rug, rubbing his eyes and whimpering, "I won't be a minute, luv. Auntie's coming with a nice bottle — and an old lady's goin' to send you some little pants — specially for you."

She picked the child up and held him in the crook of her arm, his drooping head against her flat chest, and put the teat into his mouth. After a moment's experimentation, he began to suck eagerly.

v

The shops which had survived were closed. The black-clad assistants were hurrying home, after a frantic Monday of dusting and sweeping and the resorting of stock blown off the shelves. The foreman of the rescue squad wriggled out of the zigzag tunnel he and his gang had moled into the ruins of the air raid shelter under the canteen. He took off his breathing apparatus.

"We're into it," he announced to the anxious little crowd hanging about outside. "But there don't seem to be nobody alive."

Mr Robinson's mouth tightened and Higgins threw away his cigarette end angrily. They climbed as close to the tunnel entrance as the foreman would allow them. There, they leaned on their shovels and waited. Both were covered with dust, their blackened shirts clinging to their backs with perspiration. Not by so much as a quiver did either show their agony of mind; yet Alec Robinson thought that if it were not for the support of the shovel, he would collapse. The tall, thin chauffeur took a cigarette packet out of his shirt pocket and offered a smoke to his companion. Without taking his eyes off the tunnel entry, Alec Robinson nodded refusal.

He was able to identify his wife of thirty years by the modest engagement ring on her crushed hand. The chauffeur, faced with the naked, torn body of his beloved mistress, peered in the gathering gloom at her contorted face and then at the three magnificent rings on her hands, and muttered, "Yes, it's Her Ladyship," before quietly fainting. He had to be carried across to the other side of the street by two exhausted labourers and revived by the First Aid contingent. When the body of Her Ladyship was turned over to her family's undertaker, the rings were missing.

The police reported to the constable in Toxteth that no one answering to Emmie's description had been found.

vi

It was as if the whole population was swaying on its feet. One more blow and it would, if from nothing else, collapse from fatigue. By Monday evening Gwen had decided that the Sunday night raid must be the last one; the Germans had never before raided four nights in succession; she reckoned they would not come a fifth time. If it wasn't the last of the series, she felt she would drop dead; she could not take any more.

Conor Donnelly had not helped this feeling of despair. He had slapped the children's and his ration cards on the kitchen table, as if they had come to stay another week at least. Then the doctor had arrived, taken one look at David and hurried home to his telephone, to order an ambulance; Gwen had hardly had time to wash her husband's face and hands and help him out of his dirty overalls, before the vehicle arrived and whisked him off to Walton Hospital.

"They would choose the hospital furthest away," she

grumbled to Mari, Patrick and Ruby, at lunch-time. "How'm I goin' to get out there to visit him, I'd like to know. This mornin' I'd no one to leave Michael with, so as I could go with him, to see him settled in, like."

Mari ignored her mother's whining complaints. "He's not going to die, is he, Mam?"

"Of course not," snapped Gwen peevishly. "If they can't cure a heart attack we're in a proper bad way." Her panic regarding Dave must not be conveyed to Mari.

In the afternoon, she announced to Michael, who was having a great game on the heathrug with a collection of saucepans and lids, "Now we got to go and do the ration books – yours as well – 'cos Annie's corner shop's gone with the wind. Got to find a new grocer. And all that beastly red tape, to register again."

As she trudged back home up her own familiar street, carrying a very tired and fretful Michael, she passed the pile of rubble which had been Annie's shop and she stopped to sigh sadly in front of it. The pillar box still stood amid the rubble, and Mr Marsh, the neatly uniformed postman, was just unlocking it to collect the letters from it. "Nice day," he said mechanically, and she laughed almost hysterically, "Aye, I suppose it is."

A few yards further on, she met Bridget Mahoney, her neighbour from across the road. Bridget was looking red-faced and sullen, but she listened as Gwen told her about the Donnelly invasion of her home, something she knew about already. "And to crown all," Gwen finished up, "our Emma is missing down town somewhere, and I'm worried to death about her."

Bridget regarded her dully, as she nursed her bandaged arm, cut when she had removed the incendiary bomb from the gutter of her house. Her body trembled and she could not answer Gwen at first. Then she muttered, "So's me husband – in Greece. Got a telegram just now."

Gwen was aghast, stuck for words, knowing that she should say something optimistic and comforting.

Bridget swallowed. "I don't know how to tell me boys."

vii

Conor received with some anxiety the information that Emma had not been found in the canteen's air raid shelter. The constable on duty, who had given him the news, added heavily, "Either she were struck down on her way home – or she took shelter somewhere else and got buried there."

"We could try checking amongst the unidentified." Conor sighed. "Could start with the living. I'm off duty now – I'll see what I can do on the phone."

Four unidentified women between the ages of 25 and 35 lay in three different hospitals, their names unknown, though only one had been found in a street Emmie was likely to have traversed on her way home. The voice at the other end of the telephone added laconically, "Of course, there's several hundred unidentified bodies, a goodly number unidentifiable, at Webster Road mortuary."

Patiently, Conor hitched lifts to the various hospitals; looking at the women was the only way to be certain.

One woman had recovered consciousness and had identified herself. Another had been claimed by a frantic husband. The third one had just died and Conor was allowed to view the body before it was wheeled away to the mortuary.

To see the fourth one, he followed hopefully a young probationer through a packed women's ward, filled with lively chatter. Behind a screen, a person lay on her back, arms neatly arranged at her sides under tightly tucked-in bedding. Her breath fluttered uneasily from blanched lips. Her eyes and head were sheathed in bandages, as if a white turban had slipped half way over her face. Her head was supported on either side by what Conor supposed were sandbags. An angular, elderly nurse raised an eyebrow, as Conor intruded softly.

He whispered, "I've come to see if she's Emma Thomas." The nurse nodded and stepped back, while Conor peered down at the end of a nose, prettily curved white lips and a rounded chin with an unexpected dimple in it, totally unlike Emmie's long narrow face.

The nurse's face softened, as he nodded negatively. "Poor little lass," she murmured. "It's her eyes, you know."

With a dreary ache in his heart for Ellen, mixed with sorrow for the pretty young woman he had just seen, he decided that he would try the dead.

A delivery van driver gave him a lift to within a couple of streets of his destination. He had to wait, while a calm, slender woman in a white coat dealt with a sailor in a tight-fitting Royal Navy uniform, who could not have been more than nineteen. The sailor stood timidly at the counter, his round white cap clutched in both hands in front of his chest. The acne spots stood out on his face and neck against an unnaturally pale skin. Together, he and the woman went through a series of large brown envelopes holding the effects found on or near the bodies in the mortuary. Time and again he nodded affirmatively, as he recognised the pitiful possessions. Sometimes he hesitated uncertainly and the woman put those envelopes on one side.

Conor felt himself reeling at the strong smell of disinfectant mixed with the ghastly odour of disintegrating bodies. He lit a cigarette and drew on it heavily, as he watched the pile of envelopes in front of the hapless sailor grow and grow. Finally, the woman drew the shaking boy further into the building. Conor began to whistle softly to keep his courage up; he had seen enough at the shambles of The Dwellings to understand what the youngster was going through. Thanks be to the Holy Mother that his Ellen was decently wrapped in a winding sheet in a proper coffin, and tomorrow, when his mother had arrived, they would see her respectfully committed to her own grave.

The sailor suddenly bolted past him and out of the front door. When the woman turned inquiringly to Conor, tears were streaming down her face. "He's from Seaforth," she burst out, as if she must share her agony of mind with someone. "He had fourteen bodies to identify, and some of them were a mess."

She had no trace of anyone who could be Emmie; the only likely corpse, picked up in Whitechapel, which was the continuation of Paradise Street, had been identified.

She rubbed her damp eyes with the back of her hand. "I'm sorry, Mr Donnelly. Try the temporary mortuary near the scene." She paused and tapped the table with the end of her pencil. "If I were you, I would talk to the men on the spot."

Between the mortuary and Paradise Street lay

Emmie's home. He thought he should drop in *en route* and assure Gwen that the fact that he had no news of Emmie was probably good news.

He was surprised to find the front door open and, after a perfunctory knock, he walked in.

He was immediately engulfed by his children, their faces smeared with jam, as they rushed from the tea table. They were followed by Gwen holding a feeding-bottle. Behind her, a man half rose from his chair by the fire. Robert Owen had duly received the information through the police that his fiancée was missing, and, since not much more could be done regarding the still exploding cargo of the *Marakand*, he had been given a few hours' leave. He had come just as he was, blackened and reeking of fire, his eyebrows and hair singed. When, at last, he had found a tram blundering along in the right direction, he had endured with suppressed fury the stares, and occasional giggles, of the other passengers, at his outlandish appearance.

Gwen looked inquiringly at Conor above the children's heads. He nodded negatively and she sucked in her lips as her sense of guilt returned to her. She shouted suddenly, irritably, at the children, "Now, Patrick – you kids – get back to the table and finish your tea. Now, Mike, you come to Auntie and I'll put you on the sofa, and you can show your dad how you can hold your bottle."

When the child had been propped up on the sofa cushions, he put the teat in his mouth and looked triumphantly at his father out of the corner of his eye. His father had, however, other things on his mind.

"You must be Emmie Thomas's intended," he said to Robert. "I been lookin' for her just now."

The air raid siren interrupted Conor's and Robert's conversation with the police constable they found on duty at the corner of Paradise Street.

"Oh, blast 'em," rumbled the constable exasperatedly.

Robert's heart sank, as he looked out over the enormous, smoking pyre facing him. He thought he'd seen the worst in Seaforth, but here was just such another scene of devastation – and possibly his Emmie was under it. He wanted to run across the road and start tearing it aside single-handed, to find her, but instead he had to listen to the doubts expressed by the constable that there were any more bodies there; certainly nobody alive.

High in the sky anti-aircraft fire flashed white. There were few clouds. Despite the smoke haze, it was much too clear for comfort.

From the south, where Toxteth lay, the guns spat forth. Conor, so tired that he was becoming a little incoherent, prayed in the back of his mind that his children would be spared. With a quivering match he lit a cigarette handed to him by Robert; one more flash of light was not going to help the Germans; the fires still burning would guide them beautifully.

The constable glanced uneasily at the firemen, rescue teams and a demolition squad still at work amid the destruction, and the women of the WVS mobile canteen nearby. The blue flash of the men's lanterns made them look like ghosts. Nobody ran for cover as the gunfire increased. He began to herd the chattering crowd of sightseers into a nearby underground shelter. It beat him where all the onlookers came from. He'd have thought that every man and woman in the city had enough to do at present; and if they didn't, that they would be thankful to sleep. But here they were, come to gloat. Ruddy vultures, the whole bloody lot of 'em. He blew his whistle impatiently, to summon one or two stragglers, and to draw the attention of the solitary telephone engineer, still toiling in the nearby crater.

The engineer took no notice. The whole job was almost completed and he continued to check the lines which he and his colleague had been sedulously splicing together all day. In cooperation with the exchange operators, the reconnected phones were rung in nearby offices. Sometimes the line was still dead, the telephone shattered under the debris. Occasionally, a late-working clerk or a firewatcher or cleaning lady would lift the receiver and assure him that *everyone* had gone home, which never failed to make him smile. Now, with the increasing noise overhead, he was frightened and was glad of these nasal Liverpool voices responding to him. George, he told himself wearily, you're getting a bit old for this game. When a piece of flak whizzed down and buried itself in the clay side of the hole, he clapped his tin hat on to his bald head, clenched his teeth over his cold pipe and went on working.

The constable returned to Robert and Conor and they all stared skyward. Beneath the hissing of water from the firehoses and the rhythm of the pumps, they could hear the steady chug of engines from the east, and they moved to the shelter of the sandbags surrounding the entrance while they discussed what could have happened to Emmie. The sandbags had been pierced by flak and were slowly bleeding their contents on to the pavement. Conor absently poked a bigger hole with his finger, while the constable assured him, "They cleared the shelter, the rescue squad did – they were proper tired – and then they went home to get some sleep." He turned, to rebuke someone trying to leave the shelter, and then, in answer to an impatient query from Robert, he said, "Well, you could talk to the new incident officer – the other one was killed last night."

A series of thuds not very far away announced the arrival of the Luftwaffe, and George nervously collected his tools into his tool box and said to himself, "Me lad, this is where you beat it."

He hastily had the line he had been working on rung by the operator. It failed to ring, and he cursed his wasted effort. The exchange operator said sharply, "Mind your language, if you please," and transferred her plug to another call. He made a face and was just about to remove his instrument from his ear, when distantly down the line came a hoarse female voice singing falteringly *Men of Harlech*. He grinned. The receiver must be off the hook and some cleaning woman probably dusting round it. He listened for a second; the sky directly over-head was quiet, though more distant sounds of combat warned him not to linger. The song became a series of harsh sobs. It seemed to him that very faintly he heard also the rumble of a male voice, and then, a little more strongly, the tune again sung in Welsh. He gave a small laugh. Welsh miners sang it a lot better, probably because they were always singing; he had been told that they sang even when they were entombed in a mine accident.

Entombed! My God!

"Can you hear me?" he shouted, in incredulous apprehension. There was no reply, only the weak, cracked voice carrying the tune.

He called the telephone operator. Could she heard it? But the voice had stopped and the operator told him loftily not to be so daft. Lips pursed, he put a clamp to mark the line and scrambled out of the hole. Like a lumbering bear with a tin hat on its head, he ran down the newly cleared pavement, looking madly for the constable.

The WVS volunteer, a mug of tea in each hand, directed him to the entrance to the shelter.

"Get away," exclaimed the constable, when he poured out his suspicions to him.

"I'm not joking," spluttered George furiously. "I tell you I heard it. It's possible, I tell you. And buried miners always sing – and this woman was singing in Welsh. Me grandmother was Welsh – I know Welsh when I hear it. Damn it."

"It's her," Robert interjected with conviction. He caught at the constable's arm. "Come on. Who do we have to see to start 'em digging?"

The constable swallowed, while Conor said simply, "Emmie Thomas is Welsh."

George looked a little bewildered at this exchange and they hastened to explain to him about the missing woman. "And you think this is technically possible, that the telephone fell somewhere near her and still managed to remain connected?" the constable asked the engineer.

"You've just said the canteen was on the ground floor. It wouldn't have far to fall, if it wasn't blasted

207

out; if it were protected by a wall that didn't give, like. Anyways, I heard her."

"Let's try the line again," Conor suggested impetuously. He started to move out of the sheltered doorway, but the constable held him back and pointed to the bit of sky they could see above the sandbag wall. It was filled with flashing light, and a series of reverberating booms came from the direction of the docks. "You're chancing your own lives," warned the constable. "What number was it?"

"I've forgotten. I can find out. I marked the line."

"For God's sake, let's try it," Conor urged. "Come on," he called to George and Robert. He started to run across the road, George skittering unhappily behind him, followed closely by Robert. A shrill shriek overhead sent the three of them into the gutter, hands clasped over heads, noses in the dirt.

The missile passed over them, to fall into a fire slightly closer to the river. Its explosion sent a mass of burning debris flying into the air, to start fires in buildings hitherto untouched. Firemen dropped their hoses and ducked for cover wherever they could find it, only to regroup a few minutes later and continue their tasks. Conor, George and Robert stayed firmly in the gutter until the remainder of the stick of bombs had been deposited in a neat line across the city, and had sent to Kingdom Come one ambulance driver and her assistant, twenty-two homeless people in a rest centre, two pedestrians never identified, one firewatcher and one special constable; the thin red line was becoming frighteningly thinner.

A series of bombers sweeping the length of the fan-shaped city, now dived one after the other to loose their deadly loads, and sent up fountains of rubble as their bombs scored hits. The three men cowered in the gutter, hearts racing, as all kinds of lethal odds and ends pinged and plonked on the road and pavement round them. A group of soldiers and rescue men, their hooded lanterns bobbing, chanced running for the air raid shelter. Robert heard a muffled cry, as one was hit. He crammed himself further into the littered gutter.

During a moment of lessened hubbub, Robert cautiously turned his face to peep upward. The gun flashes were like an enormous storm of sheet lightning. Tracer bullets and flares added to the scarifying display. A further beat of heavy engines made him push his face tightly against the pavement's friendly curb. George, his head near Conor's feet, stretched out a careful hand to touch the warden's boots for comfort. He could feel panic rising in him, but he was haunted by the sound of the quavering voice and he tried to concentrate on the technical arguments why he should be right. He'd *prove* he was right, he would, even if he had to dig for her himself.

In Paradise Street, a big Victorian chimney, balanced by a piece of side wall from the building in which the canteen had been, shivered and fell, its stonework rattling over the wreckage at its foot. The usual cloud of dust spumed upwards. Through chattering teeth, Conor prayed for his life to his patron saint, who had not heard from him for some years. Conor had said bitterly that he was accursed; yet even so, life seemed unexpectedly precious when it looked like coming to an end.

The Defiants succeeded in disorganising the raiders and the bombing moved further north. Robert was so stunned with noise and fright that it was a moment or two before he could make himself scramble to his feet, to find the constable bending over George, as he got to his feet, and shouting through the noise, "Come on, get back in t' shelter."

Though terrified out of his wits, George was determined. "I'm goin' to try that line again. Won't take a mo'."

"You're clean out of your mind," the constable bellowed. But he ran with them to the cavity in the street.

They crouched together in the clay hollow. George found the wire with a clamp on it. He clipped on his headphones.

"No." He found also that he could no longer contact the telephone operator.

"It could've been one of the WVS women at the corner singing," suggested the constable.

George boiled with frustration. He checked his splicing again.

Conor leaned closer to him and shouted into his ear, "I believe you."

Robert thought he would lose his reason if one of them didn't do something constructive soon. "It must've been the chimney what fell just now – broke whatever connection there was." He turned to the constable and asked, "Who do we go to – to ask for rescue men?"

"The incident officer, like I said." The constable was feeling most unhappy and cursed his indecision. He was, in principle, the ultimate authority, but he did not want to pressure the incident officer into a wild-goose chase; yet the engineer presumably knew his business. As they crawled over the gummy clay and out of the hole, he said finally, "Let's talk to the incident officer."

A curious chug-chug-chug, like a train coming rapidly into a station, made them all slide back into their refuge and hug the side of it. Not too far away, something crashed into the wasteland. Tensely they waited for the explosion.

Nothing happened.

Cautiously they lifted their heads. Again the sound of a train. Again they pressed themselves into the clay. A tremendous detonation in the direction of Exchange Station drew a string of vivid swear-words from the constable. "Now I know what we got – a bloody land-mine – unexploded. Now isn't that nice?" His sarcasm was bitter. "Blow us all into next week, it could, while we're lookin' for this woman."

TUESDAY, 6 MAY 1941

"I've never heard of such a thing before." The hard-pressed incident officer sounded kind, but he was used to survivors clutching at all sorts of straws to assure themselves that a loved one was still alive. "I think you *must* have misheard," he added to George. "It's easy enough."

"We can trace the number," George informed him coldly. "Look in your telephone book and see what the canteen's number was, and I'll trace if the line is the same."

It took a little while and the close co-operation of the telephone exchange supervisor to establish fairly certainly that it was indeed the canteen telephone line. Then, with his nose in the air, George climbed into his van and went home to bed. Let the high-and-mighty incident officer work out *where* she was.

The incident officer wasted no time. He sent for a heavy-rescue foreman, recently off a train from London, and to his surprise the man said calmly, his Cockney accent sounding strange to the men around him, "There was a case like this in London."

The plans of the buildings in the Paradise Street area, carefully prepared at the beginning of the war, had been burned with the command post the previous night, but an off-duty warden, who might know the canteen, was traced with commendable speed, through the warden of his home district; and he tumbled out of the Anderson shelter in his garden and came down on his bicycle while the raid still raged.

He could not suggest where Emmie could be, but, when asked to draw a plan of the canteen, he included the cobbled back-yard.

"Where was the phone?" asked Robert.

"It were in the kitchen at the back."

"Exactly where?"

"On a little table by the window, as I remember – though I can't be sure." He stubbed out his cigarette. "'T' window faced the yard."

"She must be in the yard, or in the wreckage of the kitchen," interjected Conor between a series of yawns. His legs felt like lead and he told himself that once they started to dig, he would go home and kip down for a while.

To Robert Owen, the dark small hours were a nightmare, while with infinite care the heavy-rescue foreman from London and a group of miners from nearby St Helen's, with other experienced people, plotted Emmie's possible position. They decided to explore whatever might remain of the light well.

Robert was sick with fatigue from the battle in No. 2 Huskisson; burns on his hands were a throbbing misery. Conor tried to persuade him to go home for a few hours, but he refused. Someone thrust a mug of coffee into his hand and he drank it gratefully. Then he insisted on going down to Paradise Street to help the rescue squad. Shoulder to shoulder with the miners, he helped to pass debris back to the road, as painstakingly slowly a new tunnel was made, to pass over the huge stone wall which had formed the back of the canteen shelter. Pieces of office equipment, beams, furniture and some precious pit-props were carefully eased into place, to hold the tunnel open. He worked like an automaton, the fear he

216

had felt when he went to the Mercantile Marine office to obtain another ship long since forgotten, lost under greater and more immediate terrors. Nothing seemed to matter now, except that Emmie be found alive.

When the All Clear howled across slateless rooftops, to be followed shortly by the first rays of the rising sun, the pace of work increased. A rotund WVS woman, a flowered wrapover pinafore covering her uniform, brought mugs of tea and a basket of fresh scones with a scraping of margarine on them. "Made them myself before I set out," she told them proudly. "We've still got gas on our side of the water."

Her face showed the same weariness as that of the rescue team, but she was so fresh and clean that Robert felt as if his mother had come all the way from Hoylake to help. "Have you heard her yet?" the woman asked.

"Nay. T' foreman's goin' to go in a bit further, now he's got a block and tackle rigged. Then he's goin' to ask the fire engines and everything to be quiet, while he listens – afore the streets get busy, like. Couldn't do it while the raid was on – no point in it, with guns and all."

She touched his arm and said comfortingly, as the weary group munched and slurped thankfully. "Och, you'll find her if she's there. You're all great lads."

Robert lifted his mug to her, his eyes twinkling suddenly. "You're great ladies," he said.

It was only when the new police constable on duty managed to organise a short period of quiet that Robert realised what a shambles of noise they had been working in. In the stillness, he was surpised to hear a seagull squawk, as it came to rest on top of the

217

broken roof of the building behind him. Not very far away, burning wood crackled, and from the direction of the river a ferry boat hooted cheerily.

The squad waited, tense as Olympic runners, while a miner as small as a jockey eased his way along the tunnel they had made. Apart from his torch, he carried a piece of piping to use as a listening device.

To Robert, it seemed a lifetime before a soft rustle and a tumbling pebble heralded the man's careful emergence. Once clear, he stood up and removed his mask; he coughed helplessly to rid his lungs of dust. His watering eyes made little rivulets through the dust on his cheeks. He nodded negatively.

Robert's teeth began to chatter. He clutched the foreman's arm. "Let me go down," he pleaded.

"No, son. You're too big."

ii

During Tuesday morning, Gwen, with Michael on one arm, squeezed into the stuffy privacy of the nearest public telephone box. It was still functioning, so she telephoned Walton Hospital.

A tired, uninterested voice assured her that Mr Thomas was resting comfortably.

Gwen determined that on Wednesday morning, she would keep Ruby home from school to care for Michael while she attempted the journey across the town to visit the hospital. She fully expected, however, that keeping Ruby home would not be necessary. Grandma Donnelly would surely arrive in time for her daughter-in-law's funeral that very afternoon, and would remain to care for her grandchildren. After lunch she must see that Ruby and Patrick were clean and tidy, ready to accompany their father to the funeral.

She had had a sharp spat with Patrick that morning about the necessity of going to school. The broken nights had taken their toll and he wanted to remain in bed. It had ended with her slapping him hard across the head and threatening to complain to the headmaster, if he did not go. At first she had thought he would slap her back, but he had got up and gone sulkily to school with the other children.

At lunch-time, as she handed him a bowl of soup and a cob of bread, she said to him, "You're a bright lad, Patrick. If you learn to read and write as good as Mari, you'll never be hungry or out of work. And I would like that for you, scamp that you are."

He had nodded agreement and lost some of his sulky look. He dreaded the afternoon. He was afraid he would cry at the funeral.

Ruby sat silent, steadily drinking her soup. She knew *her* reading and writing days were over. She looked down at the soup bowl, spoon poised, and wondered what happened at funerals. Her thin lips quivered.

A box of groceries, some children's clothing and a parcel of nappies were delivered immediately after lunch by a cheeky youth on an errand boy's bicycle. Gwen smiled. The nun had not forgotten.

A worried Conor, looking incredibly neat in a clean blue overall, washed and ironed for him by Glynis Hughes, collected Patrick and Ruby. "Their gran and me brothers' wives haven't come from Walton yet," he told a very sober-looking Gwen. "Here's a slip of paper telling 'em which church. Will you give it to them, if they come late?"

"Where you goin'?" asked Nora, held back firmly by Gwen, while Brendy sucked his thumb and stared at the funeral-goers.

"Never you mind," Patrick told her savagely. "You and Brendy go to school." Ruby began to cry.

"You stay with me, and after school we'll go down the street and buy a sweetie ration." Gwen shepherded the youngsters back into the house, where Michael was trying to feed Mari's long discarded wooden bricks to a patient Sarge.

Grandma did not arrive that day, nor did any other relation, and an extremely hurt Conor went straight back to his post after returning Patrick and Ruby to Gwen's house. "I'll try to get through on t' telephone to the warden up there and ask him to send a message. They may've got t' lines restored by now."

Once more a resigned Gwen saw her charges scrubbed from head to foot and put into bed, Michael soothed with a bottle of milk and Brendy happily sucking his brother's dummy.

"What about me mam?" asked Nora, sitting up suddenly in her white bed. "A girl at school says she's dead. What's dead? Is it like when the cat was run over?"

Gwen gulped, while Ruby shivered by her in one of Gwen's own nightgowns. Ruby's eyes were huge and imploring. Gwen said coolly, "They're still mending your mam. You don't have to worry about her. And soon your gran'll come to take care of you."

"Well, what *is* dead?" Nora insisted, as she unhurriedly pulled the blanket over herself, and Gwen tucked the sheet round her chin.

"It's when you go to Heaven," replied Gwen, and added almost wistfully, "It's proper peaceful, like, and you're with God."

"Oh, aye," replied the child, just as if they were talking about lollipops, "Sister Theresa talks about it sometimes. Do you get lots to eat there?"

Gwen laughed, for the first time for a week. "To be sure," she replied promptly. "No shortages at all."

She waited for Ruby to climb into her bed beside Michael. The girl looked drained and as hagridden as Bridget Mahoney from across the road had looked that afternoon. Impulsively Gwen bent and kissed her on the cheek. "Now you cuddle down and sleep and don't worry about nothin'. You'll feel better in the morning."

When she went into her own bedroom to see Mari, the girl was sitting on the edge of her bed, pulling off her socks. She, too, looked older than her age, her eyes black-rimmed. "I wish we had news of Auntie Emmie," she greeted her mother.

Gwen sighed. "They'll find her. Don't worry. Now hurry up and get into bed and get some sleep."

She went slowly down the darkened staircase, automatically holding a corner of her apron under the candlestick, to catch any wax before it fell on to the stair carpet.

In the living room Patrick was sitting on the black, horsehair sofa. He had his head in his hands and was crying.

She put the candlestick down on the table and held him against her apron. "Now, don't take on so, luv. She's at peace now."

She took her handkerchief from her pocket and bent and wiped his tears. He took it from her and blew his

221

nose hard.

Gwen felt as if she herself had hardly got into bed before the air raid siren went, followed almost immediately by a tremendous run of explosions. Once more, she gathered her frightened brood and hastened to the cellar steps, where, for four hours, she tried to cope with tears and quarrels, while outside a thundering tumult raged.

WEDNESDAY, 7 MAY 1941

As clerks and typists struggled over the debris to report for work in non-existent buildings, the incident officer offered to send a relief crew, to replace the men hunting for Emmie. The men refused to be relieved.

The incident officer did not argue with them. Amongst the motley gangs of workmen there was a stiff pride that they did not stop work until they had themselves carried the victims out.

An intact corner of the light well had been reached. The searchers tried listening there, but heard nothing. They did, however, find a woman's shoe and this gave them new incentive to continue.

Robert could hardly stand, but he continued mechanically to pile rubbish into skips and to lend a hand where he could. He could not identify the shoe as Emmie's.

Gathered as close as the police would allow was a large crowd of sightseers, clerks in well-pressed business suits, their female counterparts in neat black dresses with white collars and white summer hats, housewives in spring suits, with pretty baskets on their arms, and the male flotsam and jetsam of a port, who, despite two years of war, seemed to have nothing particular to do.

An untidy little office girl came out of a building still standing behind the crowd and pushed her way into the middle of the partially cleared street. She held a saucer of milk. "Kitty, kitty, kitty," she called, and, as a thin black cat sidled up to her, she put the saucer down, and explained to a young woman standing watching, "It's the offices' pussies. They got no home now." Another cat approached tentatively, and she renewed her call.

Young typists and clerks were searching the edges of the ruins for filing cabinets, account books, any records which would help to re-establish their companies, when it was agreed that a miner particularly experienced in mine rescues should go down the tunnel and decide how they should proceed further. In a moment he was gone, flicking himself along the tortuous zigzags and ups and downs, like an eel through rock-patterned water. Though the smell of this disaster was different from that of a mining accident, the dust was the same, and when he felt cobblestones under him, he paused to readjust his mask. It was surprisingly quiet, as he flashed his torch along the lines of what cracks he could see. It was clear from their angle that, further on, the yard had collapsed. This puzzled him. He turned the torch upward, to examine the fearsome mass above him. To move further in, he decided, could be dicey.

"'Allo," he called tentatively, not too loudly – it wouldn't take much to start a fall, he reckoned. "'Allo, there."

Dead silence, except for an uneasy movement overhead. Blast it. He drew his piece of piping from inside the front of his singlet and this time put it to the cobbles – afterwards he could give no real reason why he did so. He bent his ear to it and listened intently.

It seemed to him that he did hear something, a movement, other than the rustles in the wreckage bearing down round him. But it was from underneath him.

He laid his head, ear down, against the unfriendly

226

cobblestones and held his breath. Very carefully he tapped on the stones with the end of his torch.

The girl couldn't be under him? Or could she? He tapped and listened again. There was a small, strangled cry. And it *was* from underneath, but a good distance further to his right, he guessed. Taking a chance, he cupped his hands round his mouth and put his face to the stones. At the top of his voice, he shouted, "We're coming. Hold on there."

She heard him, a muffled echo. With overwhelming joy, she tried to shout back, but she had screamed so much, was so exhausted by fright, hunger and thirst that the noise was not enough for him to hear. Beside her, Dick muttered incoherently in a high fever, as if he had pneumonia.

Perplexed, the miner ran his torch again along any cracks he could find, to see their direction. He tapped the surface in several directions as far as space would allow, but there was no echo, and no further cry. He backed down the tunnel as fast as he dared, trying to imagine, as he retreated, how parts of the light well might have fallen, and into what kind of space. It had to be a cellar, he decided.

As he emerged, panting, scratched and mystified, Robert ran lightly up the debris to meet him, followed by a protesting foreman. "You shouldn't run over it like that, you fool," he bellowed. "Bring the whole mess down!" He forgot his complaints, however, when the miner said there was indeed someone there. "Under you?" he exclaimed in disbelief. "But it's a yard – a light well. Cobbled. Seen it meself when I went down a bit back."

"Well, get down there and get her out." Robert was

nearly beside himself.

"Hold on, lad." The foreman was aggrieved. "These buildings've bin blasted several times from different directions. It's not that simple." He turned to the miner again. "You're sure you heard her?"

The man smiled, his teeth flashing white in his filthy face. "I heard somebody, all right."

"Thank God!" exclaimed Robert in relief. But anguished dread then filled him. What horrifying hurt might Emmie have suffered? He fought down a wave of nausea.

The returned miner was talking again. "She must be lying in a hole under that yard. But most of the yard must be supported by solid earth – otherwise the cobbles would have caved in years ago. They'd be a dead weight."

"Some kind of arches might be supporting 'em," another man suggested. "Arches can hold up cathedrals."

"Aye, but we *could* be digging down through solid rock, if we go down through the cobbles."

"How far into the yard, measuring, like, from where you was lyin', do you think she was?" The foreman rubbed his heavy-muscled arms which ached intolerably. He was bent on pinpointing as accurately as possible where they must penetrate.

"A way," the miner said immediately. "I went over the stone foundation wall what you told me about – back o' where the canteen shelter must've been – and all me body was on cobbles. She must've been at least twenty feet from me, bearing half right; and I tell you, the voice came from below – not level with me."

Robert caught the foreman's arm. "I know!" he broke

228

in eagerly. "Me grandad told me often enough. Privateers – and smugglers – used to have hiding-places for contraband – and you said the cellar of the canteen was much older than the building above it. Could be there's some merchant's old cellar under that light well."

The foreman sighed and pursed his lips, and then said rather condescendingly, "It's an idea. But God knows how she fell into it."

"This fella here said it would be hard to go down through the light well itself. Could you still get into the shelter?" asked Robert, fatigue forgotten, and the plan of the building he had seen the warden draw clear in his mind.

"Oh, yes. It was all well nigh cleared out by the time we'd finished. Have to go down carefully, because of the of the big chimney collapsing over there, last night."

"Did you see any doors in the walls?"

"No, lad. We'd 've gone through 'em if we had – to make sure nobody was there." The tone was scornful now.

"Look again," Robert persisted. "If they had a secret cellar under the light well, then they had a place to get into it. Maybe it were bricked up when they built the offices. Round here they've bin building and rebuilding for centuries – even the offices were real old. There must be all kinds of little places built over – even small rivers have been."

The men stood round arguing amongst themselves, while the foreman thought this over. The ultimate responsibility was his and he was not going to put his men at risk unnecessarily.

Finally, when Robert had begun to think he could not bear another moment of suspense, he said, "OK. I'll go down meself and look." He turned to a young miner who was particularly small-made. "You, Evans, you can come with me."

They had been squeezing slowly round the shelter's walls for nearly five minutes, before Evans said triumphantly, "I've got it. See, this is brick, not stone."

The foreman flashed his torch along the wall. Once pointed out, it was possible to see a line under the whitewash where the texture of the wall changed. He crawled closer to the younger man and then carefully tapped on the brick and listened. No response.

ii

Some of the rescue crew, who could do nothing for the moment, went down to the WVS van to get some lunch, while, amid the smell of wet plaster mixed with that of a charnel house, the foreman dug out the first bricks with the care of a surgeon. The wall would be weaker at this point and the old brickwork could crumble suddenly under the weight of the wreckage above.

The wall proved to be four bricks thick, and when the fourth one suddenly gave and fell out on the other side, a poof of surprisingly cold, damp air blew out at them.

Evans broke into excited Welsh; then remembered his English. "The lad up there was right. There's space here." He put his face close to the hole they had made, and shouted, "Anybody there?"

In the light of the foreman's torch, his face fell. "Try again," the foreman urged.

"Anybody there?"

Very faintly came a croaking sound that could have been a human voice.

The wall was broken as fast as human hands could do it without causing a fall. As soon as the hole was big enough, young Evans wriggled through feet first. He felt around with the toes of his boots, to make sure he was not dangling over a hole. Cautiously, he stood upright.

"Lend us the torch." The foreman passed it to him and he flashed it round. "It's like a blinking castle dungeon," he reported. And then he called, "'Allo! 'Allo!"

From beyond a massive blockage facing him came a faint response, a distant sob.

"We're coming. Hold on. Are you by yourself?"

The reply was unintelligible.

Evans tried again. "Are you badly hurt?"

There was a pause and then Evans clearly heard an effort at a throat being cleared. "No," came the answer.

Meanwhile, in preparation, other men worked feverishly, pushing pit-props and tools down the tunnel and through the hole in the wall. They whistled when they saw, by the light of a powerful lantern, parts of hefty stone arches. There was room to stand against the wall through which Evans had clambered; but the rest seemed to be an almost solid mass of wreckage.

"She's on the other side of that," said Evans, his young face gloomy in the light of the lantern, as he gestured to his right.

The foreman, who had followed Evans through the hole in the wall, glanced quickly round. He said, with more optimism than he felt, "We'll find her. God, it must be five hundred years old, this place. They knew how to build in those days – and that's what's saved her, though there's more'n one fall here." He rubbed the end of his nose and then went on, "Reckon she's tucked up not far from the wall we've come through, but it's goin' to take a while afore we get through that lot."

The floor of the cellar was earthen, which at times was a help to them, in that they could loosen large pieces of debris by digging for a little way under them. Miners can almost sink into the earth when they dig, but a bucket brigade had to be formed, to move earth and debris out of the way as it was dug, and these men had difficulty in keeping up with the moling miners.

"At this rate, we'll be home in time for tea," one of them joked.

The moles themselves, though fast, moved with the greatest care, with the minimum of noise, with the least disturbance of the dense mass poised above them. A faint smell of burning made Evans shiver; occasionally small runnels of water would cascade down on them. "From the fire-hoses," the foreman told them firmly. "Water and gas is turned off. You're not goin' to drown."

Every so often the gasped curses would cease and the leading man would call to Emmie, partly to reassure her, but partly to keep them on course.

She would answer them with a faint croak. Every tired nerve alert, she had listened through an eternity of time to the muffled sounds indicating that help was coming. Sometimes the men had paused, to consider how to deal with an obstruction facing them; there was no sound, and at such times her spirits would sink. They had given up, deserted Dick and her. Dreadful, agonised fear went through her parched, starved body. She tried to shout but little noise came. She felt around the sick man beside her, to find her petticoat with which she had earlier wiped Dick's burning face. It was half under her, and she laboriously hauled it out, to suck it and dampen her mouth. Though they were lying on wet ground, it seemed impossible to do more than moisten their lips and tongues.

She found the stone with which she had tapped earlier and hit the wall unsteadily with it.

"That's good," said a voice surprisingly close to her. "Every time I call, you tap, eh?"

She tapped once in acknowledgment and prayed she would not pass out.

Outside, Robert Owen stood hunched in his Red Cross, brown jacket, nearly out of his mind with the frustration of the long wait. As he mechanically emptied buckets or handed in pieces of wood, his mind would hardly function, and suddenly he heeled over and fell face down on to a pile of debris. The watching crowd murmured and shuffled.

A First Aid man who had been checking his canisters of milk and water, and the tube which he could poke through a small hole in the obstruction between himself and a victim, and thus feed the sufferer until he was freed, dropped his satchel and ran to Robert. He went down on one knee and gently turned the exhausted man over. The doctor and driver from the ambulance also hastened across the street and together they lifted the limp figure and laid him down on the pavement, which had earlier been so sedulously cleared by Alec Robinson and Lady Mentmore's chauffeur. The lady doctor knelt to wipe gravel from his bruised face and half turned him on his side, so that he was less likely to choke if he vomited. She checked that he had no false teeth in his mouth and then lifted one of his eyelids. She smiled and took his pulse. Still amused, she got up slowly, dusted down her slacks and said laconically, "Gone to sleep on his feet."

She turned to the warden, who had come from helping the constable keep back the crowd. "Better find out who he is," she suggested, "and send him home."

"He'll be right mad if I do. It's his girl what's bein' dug out." He ran his tongue round broken teeth. "I'll get a couple of blankets and we'll lay 'im in the hallway of the office opposite."

The First Aid man returned to digging through his satchel. For the third time, he checked its contents: hypodermic syringe, pain-killers, sterilised pads, sticking plaster. A stretcher had already been carried as close to the tunnel entrance as possible. There was nothing he could do but wait. He envied Robert, sound asleep in the hallway. It was thirty-six hours since he had been to bed himself.

Far below the horrifying ruins, the miners burrowed like ferrets, thin sinewy arms flashing in the lantern light, flat-stomached bodies swinging in rhythm, as they passed buckets of earth back to a space near the broken entry to the old cellar.

Jimmy, the foreman, moved his helpers around as if he were playing a complicated game of chess, his seamed face a picture of intense concentration, as he improvised the steps of the rescue. No two rescues were ever the same; no two buildings ever fell in exactly the same way – their stresses and strains had each to be weighed up anew, and their constant tiny shifts watched with feline intensity. Not only had he to rescue those buried; he must at all costs ensure the safety of his team,

234

and as he sometimes remarked, "Me old woman would be proper put out if I buried meself and she was done out of a good funeral."

They came up within two feet of her, to a tight tangle of splintered wooden beams and what might have been part of an iron girder, the same obstruction Emmie had felt in her first search for the dripping water. Now she squeaked with shock when her foot was grasped by a warm hand slipped under it.

They were stalled.

"Sufferin' Christ!" The foreman's disappointment was as bitter as if his own daughter lay beyond the girder. "Get First Aid to bring some water and a shot for her, while we decide what to do."

The nervous young man crawled down the tunnel and fed both Emmie and Dick with water and then a little milk through the tube he thrust over the girder. She refused any sedation. Without a hint of his inward horror of the tight confinement of the suffocating tunnel, he whispered encouragement and told her that her fiancé was waiting outside.

"He's there?" Her voice was suddenly comparatively clear. "Thank God, thank God." She began to weep, soft, helpless crying in which was mingled a tremendous joy. He was there, he was safe.

When the miners were ready to start again, he backed down and told the surprised foreman that he had two living victims to get out.

Like dogs getting at a bone buried under a tree root, Evans hollowed out a space in the earthen floor under the girder. He then grasped her ankles firmly and told her he would help her wriggle down and under, on her back. When her knees were through, he grasped her bent legs and heaved her upwards. She cried out at the scratches she received, but she was through, her eyes dazzled excruciatingly by the blaze of the torch held by a second man behind Evans.

After calling Dick and getting no response, Evans turned himself on his back and squeezed himself into the space Emmie had occupied. He flashed his torch quickly round the tiny refuge, sickened by the stench. Near Dick's head, neatly wedged between a piece of stone and what looked like the remains of a table, was a telephone. So the engineer had been right. With a grin, he turned to the job of easing the barely conscious Dick out.

With difficulty, the warden managed to wake Robert. "They're bringin' her out," he said, a smug satisfaction in his expression, "and she's not badly hurt."

Without a word, Robert stumbled to his feet. Across the road he saw her being carefully carried down the slope of the debris. She was wrapped in a white sheet and strapped to a stretcher.

He pushed his way through the crowd of excited onlookers and ran across the road. Emmie was alive — and absolutely nothing else in the world mattered.

iii

On its way to Walton Hospital, the ambulance carrying Emmie, Dick and Robert, passed the bus in which a very subdued Gwen was travelling back home from her visit to David in the selfsame hospital.

Regardless of the thirty-odd other men in the ward, she had put her head down on the white coverlet of David's bed and cried. Too ill to do more than hold her hand, he had been staggered when she had laid her cheek on his work-scarred palm and told him he must get better, because she could not face life without him. She had paused to give a weepy sigh, and added, "Half the time I dunno what to do for the best."

"I'll be all right," he had whispered with an effort, and closed his eyes. It was nice to be wanted and not to be regarded as merely a walking pay-packet.

When she got home, Nora and Brendy were rolling round on the kitchen floor like a pair of angry young wolves. Patrick was kicking them none too gently in an effort to separate them, while Mari watched him from the living room, where she was seated at the table, trying to do her arithmetic homework. Ruby sat near her with Michael in her arms, feeding him from his new bottle. She was shouting, "Leave them be, Pat. They'll stop of themselves in a minute."

Gwen took one look at the fighting youngsters and total exasperation seized her. She strode through the crowded living room and squeezed quickly behind Mari's chair and into the kitchen. "Stop kicking 'em," she ordered Patrick, and he slunk back, muttering, "I were only tryin' to stop 'em."

Nora rolled triumphantly on top of a beleaguered Brendy, and Gwen bent down and administered the heaviest slap she could on the girl's small cotton-covered bottom. As quick as a cat, the child loosed Brendy and jumped to her feet. A stream of invective poured from her, as she rubbed her stinging bottom.

"Any more of that and you get no jam for tea," threatened Gwen, as she picked up the kettle to fill it from the kitchen tap. Nora made a face at her, and

Ruby hastily called the little girl to her. "You coom 'ere afore you get into more trouble, our Nora."

Brendy lay on his back and laughed, as he watched her go.

Patrick had a tin bowl of grain in his hand, some of which had spilled on to the kitchen floor in the mêlée. He squatted down and began to scoop the precious seeds together. "I were goin' to feed the micks," he told Gwen defensively.

"Aye, feed the pigeons – and you'd better do your dad's cocks, too."

After he had fed the cockerels, Patrick stood, empty bowl in hand, and looked round the familiar muddle of the Donnelly backyard. He burst into tears. Where *was* his mother? Where had she gone after death? Her body had been in the coffin the day before, but that wasn't her – not really her. Would he never again come through the back yard, to see her leaning against the doorpost, waiting for them all to come home from school? He did not know how to bear the pain within him.

An hour later, Gwen surveyed her troublesome brood across the littered tea table and prayed that their grandmother would turn up soon.

Patrick looked as if he had been crying. Deep compassion for him and for Ruby welled up in her; they must both be feeling terrible despair. Yet they were being very brave. Impulsively she leaned forward and pressed Patrick's grubby fist lying on the tablecloth. He looked up at her, startled, and saw the pity mirrored in her faded blue eyes. Quickly, he withdrew his hand and picked up his piece of bread and margarine. "Everything's going to turn out all right," she assured him, feeling a little shy herself.

He nodded.

She turned to Ruby. The girl looked crushed. She was staring vacantly at her empty plate. "Would you like another butties, luv? I can soon cut you one."

"No. I'm all right."

"Coom 'ere."

The girl rose and went to stand by Gwen's chair, like a schoolgirl called before the headmistress. Gwen put an arm round the thin body and gave her a hug and a smile. "Come on, now. Cheer up. Your gran's goin' to come soon – and I'm goin' to be next door all the time, and you can ask me." The girl smiled faintly, and unexpectedly put her arms round Gwen's neck, as she had so often done with her mother. She did not cry.

Mari watched in jealous shock. Her mother never hugged her. All she ever got was a peck on the cheek and an admonition to be a good girl. She had endured the invasion from next door, because of the strange magic of Patrick's presence. Now she wished crossly that they would all go back to their own house and that her father was home to give her a smacking kiss and call her his pretty young lady.

At midnight, she was sitting on the cellar steps, reading *Gone With the Wind* aloud to Patrick and Ruby, while one of the worst raids Liverpool had ever experienced raged outside.

On a mattress dragged down to the bottom of the steps lay Nora, Brendy and Michael, mercifully sleeping the sleep of the totally exhausted.

Gwen nodded over a cold cup of tea, while her mind went round and round in weary confusion. What if Emmie is injured – not killed? Do I have to nurse her as well as Dave? It would, she felt be a fit judgment on her,

239

for not helping Emmie with her parents; the pain-filled face of her acid-tongued mother-in-law haunted her for the duration of the raid.

THURSDAY, 8 MAY 1941

Constable Doyle consulted his notebook and then knocked on Gwen's front door. At least for this family he had good news – as far as it went.

He made himself smile as the door opened, to reveal Gwen in her dressing-gown, followed by five children in differing states of readiness for school.

"Me husband?" Gwen faltered, at the sight of the uniform.

"No, missus. Miss Emma Thomas live here?"

Relieved, Gwen replied that she did normally, but she was missing.

"Well, missus, you'll be pleased to know she's resting comfortable in Walton Hospital. Be out in a few days."

"Thank you kindly for stopping by to tell me," she began to close the door.

The constable cleared his throat. "I should tell you, missus, that we've heard as the hospital was bombed last night. We don't know the extent of the damage yet. I'll know in an hour or …"

Through white lips, Gwen murmured, "Dave!" and fainted on her neglected doorstep.

Though the constable was resigned to carrying news that had this kind of result, Gwen's collapse was unexpected. He helped to carry her in and lay her on the living room sofa. She came round within a minute or two and, through chattering teeth, asked if he or Mr Donnelly would let her know when they had more news of the hospital. "Me husband's in there, as well as Emma. I'll go over meself as soon as I've got the children away to school."

"The north end's a shambles," Constable Doyle warned. "I doubt you'd get through. I'll come as soon as I've any news." He turned to Ruby and Mari — never had he seen two sisters so totally unalike — and told them to make a strong cup of tea for their mam. "Lots of sugar in it — and see she rests a while."

ii

On the previous Wednesday, the day before the raids began, Mrs Owen, Robert's mother, had said a thankful farewell to the evacuated mother and children who had occupied her spare room for some months. "I can't stand the quiet out here a day longer," the mother had told her. "I'm goin' home to Great Homer Street."

Now, on this perfect spring morning, she asked Mr Burnett, the chemist in Hoylake village, for something she might sprinkle round the newly scoured bedroom, to kill off any vermin that her unwelcome guests might have left there. "Me daughter-in-law elect is coming out to live with me. She's in Walton Hospital at present, recovering from being buried under the canteen she worked in. Poor girl. She's real nice. I'll be happy to have her."

Mr Burnett looked over his gold spectacles. He swallowed. "Do you know Walton was bombed last night?"

Mrs Owen's hand flew to her throat. "Oh, no! Poor lass, poor lass — and poor Robbie."

She had trouble waking Robert from the sleep of the absolutely worn out. He would have to go into

244

Liverpool, anyway, she told herself, to be signed off from the *Marakand* and then find himself another berth. She sighed at the thought.

When he heard the news, he was wide awake in a moment and jumped out of bed. He seized his trousers and struggled into them.

"The phone to the hospital's dead. I tried it — or rather, Mr Burnett did."

"I can go over."

"Well, you have some tea first. The kettle's boiling." Dear Lord, what a mess he was in, too. A black eye, hardly any eyebrows or eyelashes — all singed off — likewise his front hair. And both hands bandaged by the hospital, because of the burns on them.

iii

Conor had not been home since before his wife's funeral on Tuesday. Now, on Thursday morning, after what Glynis Hughes described as a lively night but not in the usual sense, he hesitantly opened his front door. He had snatched an occasional nap at the post, but now he knew he must really sleep; otherwise, he would collapse.

On the floor of the passage inside, lay his letter to his mother, returned through the dead-letter office. A wobbly hand had scrawled in pencil on it, "Address Unknown. Return to sender". Then in brackets the writer had added, "Whole street bombed. Tried to trace in Rest Centre without success."

He stood in the narrow hall, paralysed. He could not believe it. He had been so harassed himself that he had

245

not thought about his parents' danger.

If they were hurt or killed, why hadn't his married sister, who lived in the same street, let him know?

A slow coldness crept through him. From bitter experience, he could visualise the scene so well. A dozen houses down, a whole series of families related to each other carried out dead or dying; no one surviving long enough to give names to the authorities. Those same authorities, hopelessly overloaded by the sheer magnitude of the raids, would in time name most of the victims – but not yet.

He leaned his head against his paintless front door, and cried aloud, "Holy Mother have pity on me!" He beat his fist against the unresponding wood. "I'm damned! Accursed!"

Nearly demented, he fled back to his post – and the telephone.

With some difficulty, he got through, on the newly restored line, to the wardens' post nearest to his parents' house. Then he came slowly back to his own street. Instinctively, he sought the only people left to him, his children; he turned the rapidly tarnishing brass knob of Gwen's front door and walked in.

Michael was asleep on the sofa, an empty feeding-bottle lolling by his cheek. From the kitchen came the splash of dishes being washed.

"Are you there, Mrs Thomas?"

The splashing stopped immediately and Ruby came running in, wiping her hands on a dish towel. "Dad," she cried eagerly.

He held out his arms to her. She ran into them and with his head bowed over her he began to sob helplessly. She drew back. "Dad, what's up?" she whispered, frightened by such a lament.

While she sat on his knee in the muddled room, he told her. He wept unrestrainedly, unable to hold in his despair and grief any more.

Half girl, half woman, she listened quietly, arm around his neck. Then she started to comfort. "Don't cry, Dadda. We'll manage," she said hoarsely. "Mrs Thomas'll help me – while I get started, like." She clung to him while he tried to control himself.

"I'm sorry, luv," he said, and wept on.

She was frightened to see her hot-tempered father cry, but it also put him on a level with Patrick, and she said, "Aye, everybody cries sometimes, Dadda," and gritted her teeth and hugged him closer.

When her father's weeping ceased, she said quite eagerly, "Let's go and buy a bit o' food, Dad, so as we can move back home."

That afternoon, Gwen and Mari sat and looked at each other over their teatime toast and dripping. The house was extraordinarily quiet and seemed to exude the misery of its damage and neglect. Gwen thought her heart had never been so heavy. By dint of taking three trams in a circular route and walking quite a distance, she had managed to reach Walton Hospital. The fright engendered by the bombs on the hospital had given David another heart attack. He had, however, survived, though he would need much nursing and would probably never be able to return to work. She had also briefly visited Emmie, who was heavily sedated and an alarming bundle of bandages and sticking plaster. There she had met Robert, sitting by her bed. He had told her that when Emmie was discharged from hospital, his mother would take care of her at his home in Hoylake,

247

until they were married. It was the only good news of the day. Confound her — and her furniture — she could have the lot of it.

Mari broke into her gloomy contemplation by saying brightly, between sips of cocoa, "Tomorrow's your day for Blackler's."

Gwen nodded. "It's burned down. I'm out o' work — like plenty of others."

"They might start up again," Mari replied. "You could go and see. There's probably a notice set up in the ruins, to tell the staff what to do."

"Aye. I'd be glad of a full-time job, now your dad's so poorly." Her face brightened. "I'll go this evening. People's got to buy clothes and bedding from *somewhere*."

"I'll walk down with you, if you like."

"Would you, dear? I'd enjoy your company."

iv

One of the loneliest people in Liverpool lay unvisited, except by Robert Owen, in a huge, overcrowded men's ward at Walton Hospital. Identified by the pay slip in his wallet, still in his back pocket, Deckie Dick opened his eyes on Thursday evening, to the long glinting rays of a setting sun reflected on a shiny, white ceiling. He was in a bed and shivering; yet at the same time feeling dreadfully hot. He had been vaguely aware of being bundled about, of being sponged and feeling chilled.

A face loomed over him. It was topped by a little white cap above a wrinkled brow. A pair of sharp blue eyes, red-rimmed, peered at him. His wrist was clasped by cold, bony fingers.

A misty mouth said, "He'll be all right now."

Another blanket was tucked over him. He fell asleep, only to be awakened by more fumbling hands. The air raid warning was wailing its devil's notes, and two giggling young women were lifting him out of bed. They stuffed him underneath it. "Safest place," they assured him, and wrapped his blankets round him.

"Where am I?" he asked.

"Walton Hospital," they told him, and he breathed, "Thanks be," and slept contentedly on the floor through the rest of the night.

The entire population of Liverpool had been waiting tensely for the warning to go. Some of those who still had a bed had climbed into it, feeling that they *must* sleep, no matter what happened to them. Now they raised their heads to listen. But the raid was small, short and scattered; many of the townsfolk slept through it. London became the main target, though German squadrons were beginning to regroup in preparation for an attack on Russia. In the days following, mass funerals were held, and people who thought they could not cry another tear, wept some more.

One morning, a curiously shrunken and shaky Deckie Dick, dressed in clothing supplied by a charitable organisation, tottered out of Walton Hospital and went back to the room he rented in Pitt Street. The landlady had relet it. "Ah thought you must be dead," she told him. She had, however, stored his few belongings, in case he had a relative to claim them.

Weak and bewildered, he went into a tiny café, sat down at a greasy table and ordered a cup of coffee.

From his wallet he took out a small piece of paper with an address written on it and he smoothed it between thumb and finger. The granny of the young conscript he had met in the shelter also lived in Pitt Street. Robert Owen had told him that everyone in the shelter had been killed. She must be feeling bad, he ruminated, as he slowly stirred his tasteless coffee. It wouldn't hurt him to go up and see her; the old biddy might even know of a room to let.

Ten minutes later, he was climbing the bare, littered stairs of a lodging house similar to the one he had lived in, though this one seemed to smell even worse.

He did not have to knock at the door of the first-floor front room. The occupant had heard his footsteps and had opened it a crack.

"Mrs Pickles?" he inquired of the one grey eye peeping at him.

The crack widened. In the dim light he could make out only a female form draped in a black shawl. "What d'yer want?" The voice was full of suspicion.

"Ah come about your nephew, Wilf."

A sharp intake of breath. "Well, what about 'im?"

"Mrs Pickles, can I come in and sit down? I bin ill or I'd have come before. I met your lad in an air raid shelter and promised to look you up."

A pause. "Come in."

Inside the bare, clean room, he turned to the woman. She was very small, with a pinched, thin face out of which large steel-grey eyes regarded him with sudden compassion. Her skin looked pale from poor nourishment and lack of sunshine, and was a mass of fine lines. She had no teeth. About 55 years old, he reckoned.

She said, "Aye, you are ill, I can see that. Sit down on the sofa bed. I was just goin' to make a pot o' tea and a bite of toast." She picked up a kettle from off the small fire and poured boiling water into a teapot, much blackened from being kept hot too near the fire.

Dickie sank thankfully on to the edge of the sofa; the springs complained bitterly.

"What about Wilf?" she asked. "You know he were killed? He were all I got – a real nice lad."

As gently as he knew how, he told her about the scene in the air raid shelter and of his promise.

White cup and saucer in one hand, she looked down at him, her mouth quivering. He thought she was going to cry, but she did not. She simply sighed and sat down abruptly. She took the lid off the aluminium teapot and stirred the tea vigorously.

As she handed a cup to him, she asked, "What was you ill with?"

He told her about being buried with Emmie and his subsequent pneumonia, and as he talked some of the stress went out of him.

She listened patiently, and at the end she said, "I don't think any of us will ever be the same again after all this. It's as if all our lives was overturned in the course of a week, isn't it?"

"Aye." He smiled wryly, and stirred his tea. He wondered if he still had a job. Then he burst out suddenly, "Being buried like that – it taught me life was worth having. Funny, isn't it?"

She smiled and her eyes crinkled up with a promise of laughter, when she felt better. "Have another piece of toast," she invited.

Through two pots of tea and a pile of toast, they sat

knee to knee, two lonely people tossed together by a war they did not understand.

He stayed with her for the rest of his life.

SUNDAY, 29 JUNE 1941

"It feels proper queer – to be married at last," remarked Emmie. "I thought we'd never make it."

"You mean when you was buried?"

They were wandering along Hoylake Promenade, idly pausing from time to time to watch children digging in the sand, while their elders snoozed beneath copies of the Sunday newspapers, and dogs ran yapping after balls tossed by strolling owners. It was hard to believe that, not too far from them, out to sea, men stalked each other mercilessly and that, in Europe, the art of murder was reaching new heights, while in England itself cities burned.

"Not so much being buried," Emmie replied uneasily, "Though that were bad enough. But you havin' to go back to sea afore I were out of hospital – and bein' so long in the hospital, with me nerves, and lookin' like a piece of red raddle when they took the bandages off me face; I were fit to die when I saw meself in the mirror. I thought you wouldn't want me no more."

"Tush, luv. I'd always want you. There's more to a woman than a face. Anyways, there's nothin' that time and a spot o' warpaint won't cover." He bent and kissed the top of her newly permed hair. No need to tell her that he had been nearly shocked out of his kecks when he had first seen her. But the doctors had been right. She was healing and they'd done some neat stitching on her, which they swore would fade, and the bruises on her poor body were going, too. The doctors had said it was a pure miracle that she had no broken bones and she wasn't blinded.

He tightened his arm around her waist and he saw her

wince and immediately loosened it again. Bugger the Nazis. Just wait till he got a chance at one, he promised himself bitterly. He'd never felt such boiling hatred in his life before. It bubbled in him, awaiting only the opportunity to explode.

She turned her face towards him. "I love you so," she said unexpectedly, and he was diverted immediately by a fresh surge of longing.

"Look, duck. Let's nip 'ome. Me mam and dad allus goes over to see me brother on Sunday afternoon. Let's go 'ome and have a little matinee. What say?"

She bit her lip and then grinned quite cheerfully. Why say that so much of you still ached that you could hardly bear to be touched. He'd be gone on the eight o'clock train, back to his boat and the god-damned Atlantic. She'd have weeks of nothing before he returned — always supposing he got back safe. Time enough to get herself well again — and try for a job in munitions, so she could send a bit back to the Jerries with her best compliments.